PICTURE PERFECT

DARA GIRARD

ISBN: 978-1949764499

PICTURE PERFECT

Published by ILORI Press Books

ILORI PRESS BOOKS, LLC

P.O. Box 10332

Silver Spring, MD 20914

www.iloripressbooks.com

Beneath the Covers

Henson Series

Table for Two

Gaining Interest

Careless Rapture

Dangerous Curves

Familiar Stranger

It Happened One Wedding

Unexpected Pleasure

Midnight Promise

Sweet Temptation

Always and Forever

Truly Yours

Say Yes

Picture Perfect

Clifton Sisters

The Sapphire Pendant

The Amber Stone

The Emerald Ring

Fortune Brothers

A Tempting Proposal

A Seductive Arrangement

An Unforgettable Moment

Novels

Honest Betrayal

The Daughters of Winston Barnett

Remember My Name

Illusive Flame

Winterwood Lane

Promise Me

This Changes Everything

Sparks

Piece of Cake

Dear Reader,

Welcome to the seventh book in the *It Happened One Wedding* series where the best part of the story comes after "I do."

Click!

Our lives can change in an instant.

When I started this story I had no idea how two individuals, who guarded their hearts, could meet and fall in love.

Enter a fairy tale castle, the help of a mischievous budgie and a beautiful garden.

When I mixed the elements together, plus a meddling mother and tiny lie, I came up with *Picture Perfect*.

I hope you'll enjoy Julia and Mason's story.

All the best,

Dara

You can find out more about this series and learn about my other titles on my website www.daragirard.com

CHAPTER ONE

She had him under a spell.

A dark spell.

But Celeste Borden knew she had no one else to blame but herself. She was the reason her stepson Mason had fallen for Emilia Fairbanks.

Celeste watched the couple who stood on the balcony of her penthouse suite in the waning light of the spring evening. Mason had his back to her but Celeste could picture every expression on his face, she could imagine him listening to Emilia's every word.

She saw Emilia's pretty face in profile. A face she'd once trusted. A face that smiled so innocently now as she rested a slender brown hand on Mason's arm and looked up at him with an expression that looked caring.

Celeste knew it was not.

Celeste knew that Emilia knew her power over Mason and could get him to do whatever she wanted.

The balcony door opened and the cool spring breeze

floated in toying with the vase of tulips Mason had sent her, the scent of the flowers softly drifting towards her.

She lowered her gaze when he entered the room. She couldn't look at him. Her guilt was too much.

She felt the light, warm touch of his hand on her shoulder, smelled the soft scent of his cologne, a mixture of raspberry and vanilla, which always reminded her of the sweet shop she'd loved going to as a child. "Mum, are you okay?"

"I'm fine. What about you?"

He laughed. "I'm always fine. I wish you wouldn't worry about me."

But she did worry, because although he wasn't lying to her he was lying to himself. He wasn't as okay as he liked to pretend to be. "Mason—"

"You look a bit pale. Let me have someone make you lemon ginger tea."

She patted his hand still unable to look at his face. "No, I just need to rest."

She felt him hesitate and closed her eyes hoping he wouldn't ask questions. He was more astute to her feelings than he should be. More caring than anyone in her life had been except for his father.

She briefly stopped breathing when she felt the back of his hand against her neck as he checked to see if she had a temperature. He'd been doing that to her since a child, as if having a temperature was the worst thing in the world.

Soon she felt the soft brush of his lips against her cheek. "Then rest," he said in a gentle voice. "I'll check on you later."

She nodded, keeping her eyes closed, fighting the sudden pressure of tears. *Please look after him.* That's what her second husband, Ernest, had asked her as he was lying on his death bed. It was one of the few words he could manage to say after a stroke had left him bedridden. It was an ironic ending for a man who'd traveled the world as a speaker and had been a Rhodes Scholar and worked as a researcher and clinician at the National Institute of Neurological Disorders and Stroke.

Please look after him. It was the one thing she'd promised him. And she'd failed.

And as every year passed the weight of her failure gripped her heart in renewed sorrow. Losing Ernest had been devastating, slowly losing Mason felt infinitely worse.

"Are you sure it's no trouble?" Celeste heard Emilia ask Mason as they walked to the front door.

"No, it's fine."

Celeste gripped her hand into a fist at her stepson's words. She wondered what new errand Emilia would send him on.

"You are an angel."

He laughed. It was forced, shallow but useful. It put people at ease, it was a defense he'd learned as a child. He used it even more so now. "I'm hardly that." He lowered his voice. "Look after her for me, okay?"

"There's a wedding at the castle this weekend. She's probably thinking about that."

"She shouldn't be worried about anything. Are there problems? Something I should know about? Do you need my help?"

"No," Emilia said quickly. "Nothing like that. We just stayed up late talking about details. Don't worry. Everything will be fine."

"Good."

"She's probably worried about how long you're going to live in that big manor house all by yourself."

No, no don't tell him that. Don't remind him of his loneliness. Of what you did to him.

"I'm not by myself."

"Alice doesn't count."

"I think she'd take offense to that," he said with amusement. "I'd better go."

Celeste heard the quick peck on a cheek, likely Mason to Emilia—she rarely did the reverse—then the sound of the front door closing. Once it did she took a deep breath and opened her eyes.

Emilia took a seat in front of her and leaned forward. "Mason's right, you look a bit off. Are you sure you're feeling all right?"

Unlike her stepson, Celeste felt in no mood to reassure her former daughter-in-law. She'd called Emilia over to discuss business and that's all they'd do. Mason was the only reason she still kept Emilia as an employee. In his gentle way he was able to smooth over any awkwardness that could have developed between them. Fortunately, Emilia was excellent at her job and made up for Celeste's initial misjudgment that she'd be a perfect match for her stepson. She'd met Emilia at one of her philanthropic events and been taken with her charm and wit. She'd showered Emilia with glowing praise, persuaded Mason to take a chance and go on a blind date with her and had encouraged his growing affection. In the end he'd fallen for her completely. "Is everything prepared for this weekend?"

Emilia nodded unfazed by Celeste's curt tone. Few things fazed her which was why Celeste had at first thought she would have been the perfect match for Mason. She'd been wrong. "Everything's on schedule. It looks like it will be a gorgeous wedding."

They usually were. "Good."

Emilia told her more about the event, but Celeste barely listened.

Weddings were beginning to depress her. Something she'd once celebrated and looked on with joy now gave her a heavy feeling and made tears spring to her eyes. That wasn't good since it was how she made extra income. But she knew why. She wanted to see her beloved stepson married one day, but as the years passed that possibility became less and less likely.

People looked at Mason with suspicion. Taunted him, used him. Her dear kind stepson—few would take the time to really get to know him. He'd closed his heart off and she couldn't blame him. He'd been hurt one too many times. She couldn't protect him.

Where she saw beauty others saw only darkness—from the darkness of his skin, to the inky blackness of his short cropped hair. In their quick judgment they missed the warm espresso colored eyes. Instead they focused on the menacing furrowed brows, thin lips and rough jaw. He had the same hard countenance as his father, and tailored clothing only seemed to make his features more cutting.

She'd at first been intimidated by her husband's looks, but was quickly taken over by his intelligence and charm. Their marriage had been a happy one, erasing the three years of anguish and terror she'd had to endure under the control of her first husband. A man who'd been equally as brilliant as Ernest and a lot less kind. She'd managed to leave him, taking her son Gavin with her. A handsome child like his father.

Too much like his father.

Mason had been a lot like his. Not handsome, quiet, sensitive. When she'd first met Ernest's son she'd initially been frightened. At ten years old he had the size and breadth of a sixteen year old wrestler. But with a laugh and smile he quickly won her over and she doted on him as if he were her own son. His mother had died and he easily let her into his heart.

Their family had been wonderful. Except...

She didn't like to think about Gavin in bad terms but she knew there was something not right with her son. Not right with the way he interacted with Mason.

Mason was well named. Like stone. Hard, solid. She'd found those had been good traits. He was someone she could lean on. When his father had fallen ill he was in his senior year of high school and instead of worrying about all the things that teenagers did, he'd devoted himself to them. He'd helped her pack their things so that they could return to England where Ernest had grown up. He'd wanted to be near his mother, two sisters and their families before he died.

After his passing, she returned to the house. The house that they'd bought only a year before he'd gotten sick, the one that was supposed to be their tiny paradise tucked away near a Maryland forest. It was an authentic Gothic style castle built in the 1930s. The couple who had built it had traveled throughout Europe to collect antiques and design tips to turn their castle into their own happily-ever-after.

They'd gotten theirs.

Celeste hadn't been so fortunate. She'd only started the renovations when Ernest got sick and forced her to put her plans on hold for the courtyard, tiered landscaping and stone cottage that was on the property. She had every intention of making good use of the thirty rooms. But returning to the castle after eight years away, without her husband by her side, she didn't know what to do and any thoughts of renovations had been abandoned. She didn't care anymore.

Mason had been there so that she didn't feel overwhelmed and helped her turn it into an investment property. He helped her apply for a commercial loan so that she could get the financing she needed to complete the renovations.

She'd planned to renovate the house then sell it, but with Mason's quiet, persuasive way, he'd persuaded her to let him take charge of the property and he'd turned it into a very lucrative business as a location for weddings and private receptions.

He found her an apartment twenty minutes away, which she settled into with relief, and he bought the castle. However, he made sure she profited and kept his ownership secret so that her story and face were the only things shown in promotional materials and online.

"No one wants to see me," he'd once told her when she'd said that it didn't seem fair.

She hadn't known how to respond then or now because he wasn't far from wrong.

But he'd looked after her and she wanted to look after him.

He and his father had given her so much, but she felt she'd offered little in return. Not that Mason would believe that. He told her he was fine living alone in the eastern wing of the castle. She didn't know how he could stand the sight of happy couples sharing vows surrounded by family and friends sharing in the celebration, but he told her that he didn't pay attention. That all he cared about was that the property was maintained and that the business was profitable.

He always reassured her with a smile, but she didn't believe him.

She didn't know what he thought anymore, how he felt. It was as if he were becoming more and more like stone. His kisses were tender, his touch warm, but his voice, although gentle had become emptier, his laughter hollow and his eyes...

No, she couldn't look at his eyes anymore. The pain he tried to hide frightened her.

She looked across at Emilia. "What did you ask Mason to do?"

"Oh," she said with a nervous laugh. "I need him to pick up Bonnie."

Celeste frowned. "I thought your nanny—"

"She's on jury duty."

"You could have asked me."

She waved the thought away. "I didn't want to bother you. Mason doesn't mind."

That was the problem. Mason never minded when he should. Emilia definitely had cast a spell over him. She knew his weakness.

Celeste feared he'd never know true love. That the mistakes of the past—her mistakes—would haunt him for the rest of his life. She feared he'd close his heart off to anyone else and be alone.

She had to do something. Finding the right woman wouldn't be easy and Emilia's hold was deep, but Celeste would try.

Please look after him. it had been ten years since Ernest's last breath.

She'd break the spell. Shatter the hold her former daughter-in- law now had. Melt the steel that had started to enter her stepson's gaze. She needed to find the right woman.

She needed to find someone she could trust. Someone brave, but caring. Bold, but not reckless. Someone who could see Mason for who he really was.

But she knew finding such a woman wouldn't be easy.

She needed a plan.

Maybe even a miracle.

CHAPTER TWO

T he business was hemorrhaging.

But that came as no surprise to Julia Lester since her father's photography business had slowly gone into a decline since his acrimonious divorce from her mother two years ago. Julia thought of it as the 'official' divorce since her parents had been separated for nearly twenty years (twice reconciling before breaking up again with more bitterness after each round).

Her father's business had risen up out of the rubble of September 11th. In 2001, horrified by news reports and captivated by the images that followed, her father decided that after fifteen years as a engineer he could die at any moment and it was time to go after his passion—editorial photography. He quit his job and pursued photography with a vengeance that cast his wife and two children aside.

But that was many years ago. He now paid the bills

by doing wedding photography. A far cry from what he'd imagined himself doing, but, to him, doing photography was still better than engineering. However, Julia imagined it had become difficult for him to do wedding photography with his divorce still fresh in his mind. He now thought weddings were only the entry into a hell years down the road.

She also blamed the decline of the business to a loss of clients. Her father was no longer getting recommendations from a prominent event planner who Julia had warned her father to stay away from, but he couldn't resist and that relationship hadn't ended well (to put it mildly. Julia was sure that it had only been two weeks since the woman had stopped stalking her father and had set her sights on someone else) so she no longer referred clients to him.

No matter what the reason, the business was in trouble. Julia had allowed herself to pretend it wasn't an issue. She'd officially been working for him for ten years and unofficially for nine. She'd kept herself busy with the other aspects of the business—customer service, office management, marketing and the like—and left the financials to him until she'd seen an overdue notice he hadn't managed to hide.

"I don't need a lecture," he said grim faced and ready for an argument. They sat in their tiny windowless office (the one in the basement of his townhouse she'd convinced him to create after he'd gotten out of a five year lease for a studio space he didn't need, but felt gave the business prestige) as he cleaned the lens of his DSLR camera. She glanced at his rock garden that needed to be dusted. The office wasn't elegant, but it was serviceable and within budget, which was all that mattered to her. She returned her gaze to her laptop and looked at the numbers.

Red numbers.

Blood red. They were dying. If they didn't do something soon the business wouldn't last.

She cleared her throat. She had a suggestion she knew he wouldn't like, but she had to put it out there anyway. "You could retire."

"Out of the question."

"Just listen—"

"No."

She sighed wondering if she could ever make sense with a man who colored his hair black, but kept his beard completely white. He said he was making a statement; she wasn't quite sure what that statement was. But the white of his beard was in striking contrast to his dark chestnut skin. "If the business fails you won't have a choice unless you want to go job hunting again."

He glared at her before he turned away. She knew it was a low blow. It wouldn't be easy for a guy in his mid-sixties to get hired in any field let alone one he'd left decades ago.

"You could do the business on the side and collect—"

He set the camera down and sat behind his desk looking suddenly worn. "I don't have enough to retire," he grumbled. "If I'd stayed as an engineer a little longer, maybe, but the business never made enough for me to put a lot away and the divorce didn't help either. Plus I don't want to."

She rested her chin in her hand. "Raising me didn't help matters, I bet."

He sniffed amused. "No, you basically raised yourself. I never had to worry about you. You always seemed to know what to do."

It may have seemed that way, but it rarely felt that way. Most of her life Julia felt as if she were swimming upstream. September 11th hadn't only changed the world and her parents' marriage but her sense of safety. Nothing felt clear or certain anymore.

One moment she felt as if she had a family, the next she and her sister were being split up. She was to live with their father and Myla with their mother. Suddenly there wasn't enough money, when before she'd gotten an allowance; gone were school trips and music lessons. Soon she was figuring out ways to stretch her babysitting money, cleaning cobwebs from office buildings and houses for cash, and coming up with creative ways to help her father's business get clients.

But recently she'd felt as if she was failing him. She blamed it on her own sense of boredom. She felt restless. She wanted to do something else, but he needed her and she didn't want to abandon him. She had to refocus.

He smiled. She could tell it was forced, but she accepted it as she usually did when he pretended that everything would work out. "It's going to be okay," he said. "I told you that I have the Hartwell's wedding coming up this weekend."

"I don't see a deposit."

"They'll pay when they get the pictures."

Julia jumped to her feet and screamed.

Her father stared at her wide eyed. "What was that for?"

She pointed at him. "Didn't I warn you? Didn't I tell you I'd scream the next time you didn't get a deposit?"

"Yes, but I thought that was just usually a figure of speech."

She screamed again.

He covered his ears. "Stop that!"

She pounded her desk so hard that she made her fist ache. "No! I told you that we need to get a deposit. At least *half* before the wedding and then the remainder afterwards otherwise—"

He waved his hands in remorse. "I know. I know. I'm sorry. But it'll work out. They said they'd pay. Relax."

Her voice broke. "Relax? Do you know why we're in trouble? It's not only because we don't have enough business. From the business we did get, three couples haven't paid yet." She held up her fingers. "Three!"

"They will."

She couldn't tell if he was being contrary on purpose, didn't understand or didn't want to deal with the situation. Perhaps he didn't care anymore. Perhaps he felt as trapped by this life as she did. She glanced around the room. Its soft blue walls didn't make it feel any less cramped.

She took a deep breath and returned to her seat. "You can cancel and—"

"It's too late. I told you, the wedding is this weekend."

"Exactly. We can say, if you don't pay, we won't show up."

He looked at her shocked. "I couldn't do that."

"I could."

"It's their special day."

"And they should pay for the memories. Dad, you can't keep running the business like this."

"I told you I didn't need a lecture, I only wanted your advice on what to do." He held up his hand. "And I'm not retiring and I'm not canceling the job."

Julia sighed. "Fine, I'll go after—"

"You mean contact," he said softening the word.

She sent him a hard look. "I'll *go after* the ones who haven't paid but we have to agree that from now on it's a deposit or nothing. Otherwise I won't scream next time."

"What will you do?"

She folded her arms. "You really don't want to find out."

He cleared his throat uncomfortable. "Right."

"Understood?"

He nodded. "Perfectly." He smiled at her. This time the smile was real. "I knew I could trust you to figure out what was wrong. I'd forgotten about the other jobs, they're good people. I'm sure you'll have no problem getting paid after you contact them. And don't worry about the rest. Everything will be fine, you'll see."

Julia nodded because she didn't want to worry him. Everything wouldn't be fine if she didn't do something more drastic.

Two hours later she had her suspicions confirmed when she called the former clients. One had a defunct number and the other two had similar sounding stories. She had to listen to the excuses and sob stories of why they hadn't paid. Julia had a sinking feeling it would take a lot of effort to get them to part with their money. In the meantime, she had one key option that she didn't want to use, but didn't have a choice.

Desperate times called for desperate measures.

CHAPTER THREE

Evelyn Brown could spot a blemish on a porcelain vase from twenty feet away. So when her daughter took a seat in front of her at the café where they'd agreed to meet, she instantly knew what was wrong.

"Have you gained weight?" she said, her Jamaican accent giving her words a cutting bite.

Julia sighed. "No, Mom."

Evelyn narrowed her gaze. She was a refined looking woman with cashew colored skin and black hair, stylishly streaked with silver, swept back into a French roll. Except when she was pregnant, she'd maintained the same slender frame she'd had since her twenties and marveled at her daughter's more curvy shape. "Has your face always been that puffy? I've never noticed before."

"Yes. Round face and round cheeks that's me."

"Perhaps the color of your blouse emphasizes it. I'd suggest a different color. You're more of a warm—"

Julia sighed again. "That's not why I asked to see you."

Evelyn frowned. "Please don't tell me you're here for your father."

"I could say I wasn't but then I'd be lying."

"Sometimes lying is good for the soul."

"He needs—"

"Money," Evelyn said in disgust. "And do you know why he needs money? Because he's a cheapskate. He does not dye his hair and keep his beard white for a fashion statement, it's because he's too cheap to buy two bottles."

"Mom, I think—"

"Don't be fooled, he has money somewhere. Always did. While you were doing your little after school jobs did you ever wonder how he was able to afford new equipment? Get studio space?"

"He got scammed."

Evelyn rolled her eyes. "Not hard to do with his ego."

"The business really is in trouble. I don't think he's hiding anything."

"I'm not giving him money."

"I'm not asking for money. Just a reference. You have connections."

Her mother tapped her lip with a manicured finger and feigned a pensive expression. "Let's see. Am I in the mood to use my contacts to help my ex-husband's business?" She folded her arms and shrugged. "No, I'm not. He can use his own connections."

"Mom, please."

"It's not my fault that he devoted the last days of our

marriage to growing that business and left all our friends in the dust."

"Mom."

"Especially me. All the time I gave to that man and he wakes up and turns a tragic event into all about him. He has to live his life. He doesn't want to die without fulfilling his dreams." She patted her chest. "As if I didn't have dreams too. He tells me that his life needed meaning, implying that I wasn't meaning enough."

"I'm sure it wasn't meant to be that way."

"He's free and happy now. Why would I help him?"

"You'd be helping me."

Her mother clasped her hands together and began to smile. "Work for me then."

Not in a million years. She loved her mother but could only take her in small doses. Unlike her father, her mother had done well after their separation. She'd gotten a real estate license before the separation, built a lucrative business and enjoyed the hard earned success that followed. Her sister not only had the chance to attend school trips and have music lessons, but also dance, horseback riding, swimming and tennis. Their mother had offered to do the same for Julia but she'd always declined for the sake of her father. "I like what I do."

"You're wasting your talents." She clicked her tongue, and let her gaze scan Julia's blouse and jeans. "That's probably why you've gained weight."

"I haven't gained weight, Mom. I always look like this."

"I must be confusing you with your sister."

It was meant to be a joke, but Julia never found it a

funny one. Her fraternal twin sister, Myla, had a long willowy figure, and kept her long, black hair in four large braids which she pulled into a bun at the nape of her neck. She was naturally elegant in all that she did, especially as a successful florist who specialized in providing floral decorations for large events.

Julia, on the other hand, had a full figure and was still struggling to figure out what she really wanted to do with her life. They were nothing alike in looks and even less alike in personality. Her sister never got her mother's criticisms because she always had a ready witty reply to remove the sting out of any remark. Julia always had the right remark come to her two hours later.

"Tell your father to close the business, take retirement and start dating women his own age."

She knew it best not to mention the fact that he couldn't retire yet or that the event planner, nearly fifteen years his junior, had been a colossal mistake. "He's not dating anyone right now."

"When he does then."

"What does his love life have to do with anything?"

"You're right." Her mother flashed a wolfish grin. "I just like giving unsolicited advice to annoy him."

CHAPTER FOUR

"Mom's right."

Julia nearly dropped her cell phone stunned by her sister's words. Myla rarely agreed with their mother. Julia had returned to her apartment after the chat with her mother eager to hear her sister's insight. She hadn't expected this. She sat forward on her couch and shook her head. "You are not serious."

"Not about the dating," her sister quickly clarified. "But the rest. Dad's not happy and he won't admit it. Even if you rush in and somehow save him, what about the next time he finds himself in trouble?"

"I'm sure this is not going to be a pattern."

"It *is* a pattern. Do I have to remind you every time you've come to the rescue?"

"That's not true."

"When the editorial work quickly dried up you helped him start making money through stock photography, remember?"

"Yes, but—"

"And then when digital photography came and gutted his lucrative business you encouraged him towards wedding photography. He's only managed to stay a photographer this long because of you. You look out for him and notice the trends, the changes in taste and keep the business afloat when he makes mistakes."

"It's different this time."

"I know and that's what worries me. You're not sure of anything. None of us are. He hasn't been himself since the divorce, maybe even a little before then, and you can't change that. We have to admit that he might be sabotaging this as an excuse to quit."

"He doesn't want to quit."

"He says it but he doesn't act like it. He wants you to rescue him again."

"I wish you'd stop saying that. He asked for my help and I'm giving it to him, that's all."

"For how long? Are you going to keep working with him forever? Don't you want to—"

"I'm doing small projects on the side, don't worry about me. Besides, he has a major upcoming event at some place called... Hold on a minute." Julia looked at the notes on her cell phone. "Right, it's called Wendhaven castle."

Her sister burst into laughter.

Julia frowned. "What's so funny?"

"That's a good one. I really needed a laugh today. Okay, no really. Where is your next wedding shoot?"

"I *am* serious. He told me that the Hartwells are getting married at Wendhaven."

"Oh poor Julia. I can't believe you fell for that. There's no way."

"Why not?"

"There are only twenty- events allowed at that place each year. I heard the owner charges an enormous fee and then gives the couple a choice to donate half to one of seven charities of their choosing, making the couple feel altruistic as well as lucky. For the send off you can't throw rice only waste-free bird food or bubbles. The owner is eccentric and mysterious. How would Dad get to know anyone who would get in? Where did he meet them? Did they contact him? How did they find out about him?"

"I don't know."

"Anyone who can afford a wedding at Wendhaven must have money. How much did he charge them?"

"Enough," Julia said not wanting to admit that they hadn't gotten paid yet. "I believe him. Dad has the placed listed here."

"Maybe it's misspelled."

"He said it was a game changer."

Her sister swore. "Really?"

"Yes, so I have to make this work."

"No, you have to get Dad checked out right away. He's clearly delusional."

"Myla."

"I mean it." She lowered her voice. "I know two people who have tried every way you can think of to get an event there and have failed miserably. I'm telling you, no ordinary person gets a wedding there. You have to fill out an application and the requirements change. No one knows why one couple gets selected over another."

"Yes, well—"

"And you're trying to tell me that our father with his little dead—"

"It's not dead yet."

"Photography business has gotten in?"

"It's not him, it's the couple. They're the ones getting married. Maybe they have connections. I don't know. But look, the worst that could happen is that we show up and they tell us to leave. But I'm not going to question him about it."

"There's also another risk."

Julia stifled a groan. She didn't need to hear any more bad news. "What?"

"What if it's a test and Dad fails and then it ruins his reputation for years to come?"

"That's not going to happen. Besides," she quickly said before her sister could continue, "Dad is good at what he does. Nothing bad will happen."

"For your sake I hope that's true."

HER SISTER'S warning made her nervous. Julia rested on her bed that night unable to sleep, wondering if there was anything she was missing. An opportunity she wasn't considering. If the couple paid and the job was as grand as her father said then this event would help their reputation as well as help them pay the bills they owed. They could show what they were capable of.

If it worked.

She usually didn't get nervous, but she felt out of

touch. She'd never heard of Wendhaven castle or its eccentric owner.

She left her bed and went online but couldn't find as much as she wanted. All she saw was the magnificent building, scant information about the owner—a woman who opened the castle for weddings and special events in memory of her dear, departed husband. There was also some information about her family, she spoke affectionately about her sons Mason and Gavin who both traveled extensively on behalf of various causes, but nothing of much interest. Most of the information was what her sister had told her. The demands, exclusivity.

Although the site listed the charities she donated to, Julia had a feeling there was much more to Celeste Borden than she shared. There was a chilling beauty to her smooth nutmeg skin, delicate features and perfectly styled, short black hair, but all her actions of supporting various charities and the glowing praise about her work with them suggested a warm heart.

Julia had to make sure that her father could do the job and not ruin this woman's reputation or their own.

And it would have been a perfect day if her father hadn't suffered a full on panic attack.

CHAPTER FIVE

"I can't do this. I don't know why I said yes. I'll be ruined if anything goes wrong—"

"Dad...deep breaths," Julia said. She stood in her father's living room among the camera equipment he had yet to put in his blue Ford Mustang. Only an hour ago she'd called him to make sure he was on schedule and discovered he was in the middle of a meltdown. "You'll be fine. I'll be there with you. You've done this a lot of times."

He shook his head. "Not at a place like this. Not with people like this."

"Okay, Plan B. Since they didn't pay their deposit there's still enough time. I have someone who can be a replacement for us. She owes me a favor and...what was that?" Julia asked when he mumbled something.

"Their deposit hit my account this morning."

"That's great let me see." She looked at the amount. Her heart grew cold. She'd never seen a number like this before. "Dad, how much did you charge them for the photo package?"

He sent her a look like that of a naughty child. "You told me to raise my rates."

She pointed to the screen on his cell phone. "This is three times what we usually charge!"

"I wanted to get better clients. I really didn't think they'd go for it."

"Where did you meet them? *How* did you meet them?" She waved her hands. "Never mind. It doesn't matter now. You have to do this. You can't accept this kind of money and not show up."

He covered his face. "I know. But do you know how much—"

"Dad, if you don't go, you'll be sinking us. You'll be not only ruining the business but ruining their special day. A day they've been planning for. Don't leave them with the memory of the wedding photographer not showing up. Today you're going to capture their special memories and give them—"

He grabbed his chest. "I think I'm having a heart attack."

"You're not having a heart attack. The doctor told you to—"

"It hurts so bad." He slid to the floor. "I can't do this. I should have canceled. I shouldn't have thought of the money. I got desperate, greedy. This is my punishment."

He curled up into a ball.

Julia sighed. He'd had these moments before, but this was a bad one that she couldn't resolve in two hours.

She went to the kitchen and grabbed a knife then

returned to her father and took his hand. "Oh, dear. Look at that. You cut yourself." She sliced the knife across the fatty part of his palm, enough to draw blood, but not enough to injure veins.

He cried out in pain and stared at her wide eyed. "What did you do that for?"

"Let's clean it up," she said in the same neutral voice. "Too bad you won't be able to hold the camera. I'll have to do it for you and you'll be my assistant."

He stared at her as she bandaged the wound. "Couldn't you have just pretended to wound me?"

She shot him a look, waved the knife and said in a low voice, "Right now you're lucky the cut was shallow."

"You can be scary sometimes."

"Better scary than useless."

He had the grace to look embarrassed. "I'm sorry about this."

She sighed regretting her words. "Never mind."

"If your mother—"

"Don't blame her for this."

"I used to have more confidence. She took that away from me. You understand that, right? I wasn't always like this."

No, sometimes she wondered if she knew her father at all. Before their lives changed, he'd go to the office, come home, and look at her homework. He was fun, a little distant, but she hadn't expected much. When he'd left engineering to pursue photography, she was a freshman in high school. She didn't care about the long hours, that he spent most of his energy learning his craft, searching for clients, building his business. He seemed more alive then, not as distant.

She wanted her parents to be happy.

The divorce hadn't been a shock. Unfortunately, her father had been stunned, strangely hoping for another chance at reconciliation. He hadn't wanted to believe that his life with her mother was finally over. That the separation would become permanent.

Her sister listened to their mother's woes while she listened to their father's. She'd been listening ever since. For the past two to three years, the man who'd once taken pride in his work could dissolve into panic at the least provocation. He could be reckless one moment, cavalier the next. But she knew he was dealing with the final loss of the life he thought he could regain. Despite his flaws, he was a good hearted man. She wanted to protect him from anymore hurt.

She knew what being hurt felt like. She knew what it was like to bury a dream.

"This is better," she said taping up the bandage. "The blood makes it more real."

"Thanks for this."

She only managed to smile then walked outside and looked up at the clear blue sky. Her heart pounded. She could feel her own grip of panic. She didn't do photography. Not like this. She'd studied. But she hadn't done a professional job in years. Certainly not a wedding.

Fortunately, she was passable with the help of editing software, which would be her saving grace. If she goofed, she'd find a way to cover up every mistake.

She closed her eyes and took a deep breath. She'd

find a way to get through this. The problem was that she'd have to think like her father. Their shooting styles were so different.

She always captured the wrong thing, always looked at what other people missed. She saw beauty in the strangest places. That was what her instructor had told her. The reason why she'd given up on her dream...

But she wouldn't do that. She wouldn't make that mistake. She'd learned her lesson. She'd be normal. Photograph normal things. Think through the eyes of the bride and groom. She'd look over her father's notes, see what the client shots would be and make it work.

Like she had her entire life.

CHAPTER SIX

A fairy tale.

Those were the first words that came to mind when they drove up to the magnificent structure. A castle tucked in the gentle embrace of a Maryland forest, standing proud in its magnificent, ornate grandeur. She wouldn't be surprised to hear birds singing and possibly catch sight of a trail of fairy dust on the rows of pale pink, yellow and red roses that lined the main gravel path. The sight took her breath away. She could see why couples scrambled for an opportunity to get married here.

She'd have to capture the bride and groom in the garden, perhaps children scampering along the path, the light of the sun touching the tips of the trees.

"Remember this is important."

Her father's words brought her back to reality. She had to do things traditional. She couldn't afford to get off script. She sighed. She would have to see if she could get a chance, even if it were for ten minutes, to capture something unique. She doubted she'd ever get a chance to take pictures in a place like this again.

She'd practiced in her head what she'd tell the couple when they arrived. She'd already managed to allay the fears of the wedding planner, a woman as skinny as the chain that held her glasses around her neck and big green eyes. The woman had halted their progress to the main house like a security guard when she'd spotted them with all their gear.

"My father injured his hand, so I will be assisting him. Rest assured, we will stay on schedule and won't get in the way." The wedding planner seemed pleased with Julia's ready response and hadn't bothered them since.

But that didn't seem to stop her father's anxiety. He kept asking her if she remembered the extra camera, lenses, if she'd looked over the client's shot list. After the fifth time he asked her to check the lighting she said, "What has gotten into you?"

"This is a big deal."

"I know it."

"No, it's more than...never mind."

"It will be fine." She didn't know why he was so jittery. The weather was ideal, the lighting perfect but something made him anxious. Unfortunately, she knew being angry with him would only make it worse. They stood in the Great Hall where the couple would soon join them. "Sit here and relax while I scout another location."

"Don't go too far. There are places off-limits."

"Relax, I won't go into any locked rooms." She smiled, but her father continued to look worried. "I'm staying outside near the courtyard."

"Good."

But she lied. She initially went to the courtyard, its lush greenery filling her with delight, its beauty awe inspiring. Only a few yards away she saw a stone cottage that looked like it belonged in an enchanted forest. But then she saw another part of the castle that housed a garden. One she'd never seen before. It was both wild and tamed at the same time. Beautiful and beastly. Such a strange intriguing combination. A different vision. This location hadn't been shown online. But it was one of the most striking things about the place. She couldn't help but take two pictures before she remembered herself and returned to the Great Hall.

SHE HAD at least three 'Uncle Bob's', guests who kept getting in the way of key shots, she had to deal with.

Ten hours carrying around twelve pounds of equipment could be tiring but Julia barely felt it. Evening had settled over the castle and she saw it in another light. She'd had to stop the family from wanting more pictures on the balcony, not that she could blame them, it was an extraordinary view, and usher them to the reception.

She sent her father home and did the remainder of the event herself until the couple drove away in a sea of bubbles.

Everything went on without a hitch.

She was alone in the main hall and had just put her camera bag on her shoulder as the cleaning crew began their duties when she heard the fluttering of wings. She looked up and saw a little grey budgie sitting on a railing with a blue string tied to its leg.

"What are you doing there?"

The bird whistled a catcall in response, surprising her with the sexually suggestive sound. She wondered where it had learned it from.

She slowly climbed the stairs. Was it part of the wedding party? Had it gotten lost? Was it a wild bird that had gotten its foot caught in one of the decorations? She would hate to leave it only to have it fly away and get entangled in some tree with no way to escape.

"I'm not going to hurt you," she said in what she hoped was a soothing voice. She was only a few feet away and felt triumphant that she could grab it when the bird flew out of reach. "No, don't..." She hurried after it down the corridor up another set of stairs, into a room and out again then down the stairs and up a spiral one and was about to give up when it flew into a smaller room. She closed the door behind her so that it couldn't escape. "Gotcha this time." She crept closer and gently grabbed the string.

"You seemed to have tired of our little game, huh?" she said surprised by how easy it had been to finally catch it.

The bird blinked and whistled the catcall again.

"You are a little cutie. Are you friendly?" She hesitantly touched it belly and it closed its eyes in pleasure. "Okay, first I'll see if you belong to one of the staff or perhaps one of the guests forgot you. If not, I'll have to see what to do with you. It's very dangerous for you to be flying around with this string attached." She went to turn off the light, but stopped when a tiny star burst of light caught her eye.

She walked closer to see where the source had come from and saw a soft ray of moonlight perfectly touching the rim of a champagne glass. "Okay, my little friend, you're going to have to wait a bit," she said tying the bird to her camera bag so that it couldn't fly away again. "I have to capture this." She lifted her camera and took the shot.

"You're not supposed to be here," a deep voice said, emerging like a soft growl among the shadows.

"No, don't turn around," he said.

Julia froze, her throat tightening. She hadn't heard the door open or anyone enter. "I apologize. I didn't know."

"Or didn't care." His voice softened. "No, I said don't turn around. Stay exactly where you are."

"Are you with security? I wasn't stealing anything."

"Isn't taking unauthorized photographs a form of stealing?"

Fair enough. "I'll delete it."

"No. There's no need." She felt him move behind her, smelled the faint scent of raspberry, vanilla, perhaps a little lime and something else. Something she couldn't quite place. Something alluring that caused goose bumps to scatter across her skin. The scent of longing...desire. Whether it was his or her own she wasn't sure. She certainly felt a strong desire to know who he was, to see his face not just sense his presence, hear the sound of his voice. Was he a man to be desired or feared?

She licked her lip. "If you want me to leave I'll have to turn around."

"What's your name?"

"What's yours?"

He paused then said, "I asked you first."

He had the advantage. She could quickly spin around and see who he was, but what if he had a gun on her and she startled him and it accidentally went off... shooting her in the side...she'd fall to the floor, bleeding...loosing grip of her camera and she'd watch helplessly as it fell to the ground...get its lens cracked...

"You don't know your name?"

Julia pushed the grisly image from her mind as she gripped her camera closer.

"Julia Lester. I'm the wedding photographer."

"I thought that was..."

"I'm helping him. I'm his daughter."

"I see. Does he know you're snooping around here?"

"No, and I wasn't snooping. Honestly, I followed this bird," she motioned to the budgie, "and ended up here."

"Why would you follow a bird?"

"I thought it might be lost or belong to one of the guests and I hated the thought of it getting caught in the trees or something. I wanted to return it to its owner."

"I see. Now explain the picture."

"The picture?"

"You've explained how you ended up in this room, but not why you were taking pictures."

"Because of the light."

"The light?"

"Yes." She knew it would sound silly, but he had asked. "The moonlight was so lovely and I saw that champagne glass and had to capture it."

"I see."

She cleared her throat. "Do you need to see ID?"

"Not yet."

When he fell silent she cleared her throat again before she said, "Can I—"

"What was that song you were singing?"

She'd been singing? "I don't..." She paused then remembered she tended to hum when she was happy. "Oh, it's nothing."

"Tell me anyway."

She felt her face burn. "It's a song by the Du Tones a classical rap group."

"Classical rap?"

"Yes," she said feeling a little defensive. "A quartet of classically trained musicians and a rapper. Their work is quite good."

"An interesting mix."

"I like things like that. Strange mash ups, objects people don't think belong together."

"Hmm. Like moonlight on a champagne glass?"

"Yes."

"Did you take a picture of the bird?"

"No."

"Too ordinary? Plain."

"No," she said surprised by the question. "I didn't get a chance."

"Why not take one right now?"

"I really should return—"

"It won't take long."

She lifted up the camera and took a snapshot.

"Now you can untie it."

"But—"

"Alice isn't lost. She's just being naughty."

"Oh, she's yours?"

"She belongs to the house."

He made a reassuring clicking sound and the budgie responded with the catcall whistle.

"Did you teach it that?" Julia asked.

"No. Someone else did."

"Someone with a naughty sense of humor."

"Hmm." He cleared his throat. "Could you hurry it up? She'll start getting anxious being tied up."

"Oh right." Julia rushed forward and quickly untied the bird that immediately flew behind her. She didn't dare turn to see where it had gone. "I didn't know."

"If I'd had my way you still wouldn't, but it can't be helped." He paused. "Do you only do wedding photography?"

"No."

"Do you have a business card?"

"Yes, but I don't give my card to strange men who won't identify themselves."

"Okay." She heard the sound of soft cloth brushing against fabric then felt him close behind her again. "Here."

She looked to her side and saw a black gloved hand holding out a crisp white business card. The image was strange. Black gloves made her think of burglars or stranglers or murderers. But a murderer wouldn't be handing her his card, would he? She took the card then paused when she saw the name. She gasped. "You're not supposed to be here."

He chuckled. "Why not? It's my stepmother's property."

"I didn't mean it like that. I mean you're supposed to be abroad. That's what it says online."

"Well, I'm here now." He held out his palm face up. For a moment she wondered why... He had such a large hand. He was a big man, she could sense it from his presence behind her and his hand confirmed her suspicions. But after staring at it, almost mesmerized for a moment, she finally realized he was waiting for her card. She suddenly felt nervous. Why would he want it? "I wasn't trying to spy or snoop, honestly. Please don't tell your mother. I know she's very particular about things. It's just this place is so beautiful and I wanted to capture a moment that the couple could remember."

"Uh-huh."

He didn't believe her and he had no reason to. She hadn't taken a picture of the glass in the moonlight for anyone else but herself. With trembling hands she found her wallet. She'd told her father everything would be fine. Things couldn't be ruined at the last moment. "I wanted to compliment your mother on her garden near the stone cottage. It's stunning. You really should include it in your marketing material. Although people aren't allowed inside the cottage, couples could take fabulous pictures outside in the garden."

She felt him pause and wondered if she'd said something wrong. "Don't worry, I only took the required shots. The couple didn't want to be too...what was the word they said? Spontaneous. They didn't see the garden the way I did. Thought it was a little too wild." She pulled out her card and placed it in his palm. "But I thought it was beautiful."

Silence greeted her words.

She turned around expecting to see him gone. But he wasn't. She suddenly faced a broad chest dressed in an evening suit. She gasped in surprise but before she could raise her head and see his face, she heard a soft growl of annoyance before he darted to the side, a dark form hidden in the shadows.

"You can leave now," he said before she felt him leave the room and heard the fluttering of wings follow him.

CHAPTER EIGHT

"Don't say it," Mason said to the little budgie that had landed on his shoulder.

"Garden," the budgie said, one of the few words it liked to repeat.

"I said don't say it. It doesn't matter what she thinks."

But he was shaken. Truly shaken. No one had spoken about his garden like that before.

"All that matters is that you didn't get seen by any of the guests." He returned to his study annoyed that his heart pounded more than it should. His breathing wasn't quite right either. "It's because I was worried about you," he said to Alice as he returned her to her large cage. "I'd been looking all over."

But that hadn't been quite right. He'd noticed Alice flying in the hall and had been about to call her back when he'd noticed Julia.

Julia. It almost hurt to say her name, even to himself,

because saying her name made him feel like he knew her when he knew nothing about her. Nothing except that she had a nice hourglass figure, pretty brown skin and straight black hair she pulled into a ponytail, that she liked to hum classical rap songs, that she thought budgies were cute, that she was a wedding photographer who liked to take pictures of inanimate objects and that she thought his garden was stunning.

He took a deep breath. What had possessed him to give her his card? She'd been nervous enough, he'd been lucky she hadn't seen him. He keenly remembered the sight of her trembling hands as she handed him her card, but he'd wanted it. He'd wanted something to remember her by. It was a foolish fancy.

He took another deep breath. This wasn't like him. He hadn't been this attracted to a woman since...

It was the shock of Alice's empty cage, his fear that she'd cause trouble, his worry that he wouldn't get to her. That was why he hadn't acted like himself. And he'd also been worried about his stepmother. She'd been more out of sorts than usual. Her phone calls had become cryptic and he couldn't figure out what was wrong. Their last conversation, only a few days ago, still bothered him.

"Don't let Emilia use you," she'd warned him when he'd called to make sure she was okay.

"She's not using me," he replied surprised by the force in her tone. He sat back in one of the chairs in his study that gave him the most comfort, but his body suddenly felt tense. "We're family in spite of what happened and there's Bonnie."

She sighed. "Yes, Bonnie."

"What's wrong? I thought you liked Emilia."

"I do like her. I wouldn't have her working for me if I didn't, but...you can't let her depend on you too much."

Mason leaned forward and forced a laugh. "It's no trouble."

She sighed again.

"Mum, would you like to travel? To get away? I can schedule—"

"I wish it were your wedding day."

He paused. "What?"

"This weekend event. I wish—"

He trailed his hand along the edge of his desk, feeling the smooth wood against his palm. "Don't."

"You have to think about yourself."

"I do."

"You've been alone ever since—"

"I'm fine. It's better this way."

"I know I made a mistake once, but if you'll let me—"

"You didn't do anything wrong." He ran his hand along the edge of the desk in the opposite direction, this time with enough force to make it feel as if the wood was burning his palm. He kept his voice neutral. "It's me. If I really wanted to get married I could. Every woman has a price."

"I would want you to marry for love."

"Love can be overrated." He hesitated. "Not everyone can be as lucky as you and Dad. You managed to find each other."

"I want the same for you."

He sat back and repressed a frustrated sigh. She

wanted too much for him. That was the problem with her. She had been a wonderful, indulgent stepmother and she didn't realize that she couldn't give him everything. He didn't want her to feel guilty about a past that she couldn't change. "I know, Mum. But I'm all right now. Let me treat you to dinner."

"Another time."

"Don't make me wait too long."

But days later she still hadn't given him a date.

He'd call her tomorrow to see what she was up to. He didn't want her to worry about him. He didn't know why she did. He kept his troubles to himself. He was fine alone. He'd gotten used to it. It hurt less than desiring a life he knew he'd never have.

He didn't help Emilia because he had to, but because he wanted to. He still wanted to be close to her even though he'd lost her heart. He wanted her to depend on him so that he could matter to her even in the smallest way.

It was pathetic, but it was better than nothing. They were friends. That was the best way he could look at their relationship. Not everyone could understand that, but he didn't have many people in his life either. People usually wanted something from him. But he'd grown used to that and kept them at a distance, unless they proved useful.

With money and position he could find someone who would marry him, but he wanted more. He wanted someone who wanted him, not just what he could give.

Perhaps in another decade he'd surrender to a loveless marriage. In the meantime he'd surrender to unrequited love.

He took Julia's business card out of his pocket and placed it on his desk. He sat and stared at it still wondering why the sight of it excited him in a strange way.

He gripped his hands together and softly swore. It wasn't Alice or his mother that had truly shaken him. It had been her.

Julia Lester: A photographer who enjoyed taking pictures of beautiful things.

He opened his desk drawer, tossed the card inside and closed it with such force that it startled Alice who flapped her wings in alarm.

He looked at the budgie in regret. "Sorry."

She mimicked the sound of a cuckoo clock in response.

He stood, regaining control of his emotions. She'd shaken him a little, but now it was over.

Except that it wasn't. He couldn't stop thinking about her. He couldn't stop being curious to find out more. So ten minutes later, after trying to read a trade magazine he couldn't focus on, he pulled her card out of the drawer and looked up the website she had posted.

What he saw didn't make his heart pound. It made it hurt. How she combined photography and digital art was breathtaking, alluring, seductive.

She saw the world in a wholly different way. Some of her works were stark black and white pictures with little adornment, but the full color studies where she added an artistic flair caught his interest the most. She could take ordinary objects like a discarded plate left on the side of a cornfield and make it look like something of exquisite beauty.

He briefly closed his eyes taking control of his emotions before he opened them again and ripped her card in two.

He dropped the pieces into the drawer and closed it; as efficiently as he closed his traitorous heart.

CHAPTER NINE

"Where are you?"

Julia closed the trunk of her car wondering if she should have answered her father's call or just let it go to voice mail instead. "I'm almost home."

"You should be home by now. What were you doing? I thought I'd hear from you by now."

"I was getting some other shots," she said not sure she should elaborate. *I sort of met the owner's son* didn't sound right and she didn't want to explain that she'd gone to the section of the castle she shouldn't have. Her father was anxious enough.

"Do you think you got everything you need? Did you go over the client shot list?"

"Yes."

"Twice?"

"Five times."

"You're lying."

"Would it make you feel better if I said no?"

He sighed. "Julia, this is serious."

"I haven't ruined your reputation. They will be pleased and once I'm in front of the computer I'll make real magic happen."

MAGIC. That was the word that came to Julia's mind the following day as she worked on the wedding photos. There wasn't as much touching up of the images needed as she'd feared. A blemish here, an unwanted background image there, but overall it had been an easy shoot.

But then...

Then she came upon the images of the champagne glass lit by the moonlight. Somehow it was perfect. Few things were, but this image, captured so recklessly, was and she thought of him.

The dark gloves, the voice, the man who hid in the shadows. Why would the owner's son do that? Perhaps it was some delusional person trying to impress her? Business cards were easy to make. But what could he possibly want with her? She wasn't wealthy and didn't have connections.

She pulled out the card and looked at it. She could send him the images. Just to show good will. That she hadn't been lying.

She dashed the images off to his email address.

Minutes later she received a reply.

Not bad. Alice says they're excellent.

Julia stared at his note for a moment, her heart racing. First, she was stunned that he had replied so fast. Second, she was surprised he'd replied *at all*. And then she was annoyed. *Not bad?* Was that supposed to be a joke? She pulled out her cell phone and sent him a text. *Very funny.*

I'm serious. Alice tends to exaggerate.

I agree with her. They came out perfect.

You're the expert. Can I see more?

She paused. Why would he want to see more? *You can go to my website.* Although she no longer took pictures for fun she still maintained the site as proof that she'd tried and failed. The images there represented the most basic of her work.

Already been there.

Her heart wouldn't stop pounding. She wasn't sure if she should be afraid or excited. Why was he interested in her work? Why did the thought of him looking at her portfolio on her website make her mouth go dry? What did he think? Did he find her pictures odd or boring or amateurish? Why did she care?

She swallowed. *So how much more do you need to see?*

I have an insatiable appetite.

Then I can't help you. I like my work to be appreciated not just devoured.

I'd like to hire you.

Her palms suddenly felt wet. Was he getting married? Did he need a wedding photographer? Would she have to pretend to shoot pictures like her father? Why would he choose her?

I don't really do a lot of wedding photography.

I can tell by your site. I don't need you for a wedding.

Why did she feel so relieved that he wasn't getting

married? She briefly closed her eyes. It didn't matter. This was a great opportunity. *Okay.*

Are you free Thursday at ten a.m.?

Sure.

Good. See you then.

CHAPTER TEN

"You can't go back."

Julia resisted the urge to bang her head on the desk. She and her father sat in their office while a steady drizzle of rain tapped against the house. She'd shown her father the wedding photos and he'd selected the ones he felt were the best. The activity had calmed his mood until she told him about her upcoming visit to Wendhaven. "Dad, this is a great—"

He shook his head, adamant. "It's not a good idea."

Julia sat back and folded her arms. "Dad, what's really going on? You've been jittery ever since this job. Is there something about him you don't like?"

He bit his lip. "It's not that."

"What is it?"

"I owe them money."

"Who?"

"Wendhaven."

She paused. "That doesn't make sense. How can you owe them money?"

"It's a long story. I haven't been able to pay them back yet."

"How much?"

"I needed to prove myself."

"How much?"

"You know how much it costs to start up things?"

She folded her arms. "Fine I'll call him and ask."

"Seventy-five thousand."

Her arms fell to her sides. "That's impossible."

He hung his head. "I'm afraid it's not."

"How on earth—"

"It's a long story."

"Then make it short!"

He smoothed out his beard. "I was desperate for work and the couple seemed so heartbroken, I wanted to help them. They didn't have an event planner or anything. They were babes in the woods. So I managed to convince the owner of Wendhaven to give them a chance. I heard that she liked love stories and wrote her. I didn't think anything would come of it, but to my surprise she was willing to meet with me to hear more. Or at least one of her associates did. And I told her the couple's story and she listened with tears in her eyes, then said she'd get back to me.

"I really didn't think much of it until I got a call that they would like to give me and the couple a chance. I said I'd cover the expenses because the groom said his money was tied up."

"But how could it come to seventy-five thousand?"

"I didn't know much about weddings really so I got the full Wendhaven package that included all that a couple would want. They had so many guests to feed and there was the rehearsal dinner, the bride needed a dress so they suggested a wedding boutique..."

Julia sighed. "Dad."

"The couple promised to pay, the groom showed me his business card and when I went to the website it looked amazing. He was the CEO of—"

Julia shook her head, saddened that her father could fall for such a scam. "Dad—"

"So I organized everything and..."

"They didn't pay you," Julia finished.

"They disappeared with the photos and everything. I never thought I'd have a reason or chance to go back to Wendhaven so I pushed it from my mind. But I still owe them."

Julia closed her eyes and said in a low voice, "How long ago was it?"

"Please don't scream."

"How long?"

"Nearly three years." He shrugged. "She hasn't come after me so perhaps she's forgotten."

"I don't care if it was seven! You don't forget that kind of money."

He shrugged. "She's rich. It probably didn't matter much to her."

"You should have told me. All this time I thought...where is it written? This debt dwarfs all the others."

"That's why I didn't want to tell you."

"How were you planning on paying it back?"

He lowered his gaze. "I don't know."

Julia buried her face in her hands and sighed.

"So now you understand why you can't go back and see him. His mother might have told him and he might use you."

"That wouldn't make any sense. I don't think there's anything about me worth seventy-five thousand. But—" She held up her hand before he could speak. "If he wants to use me as a sex slave, which would be truly laughable, it would be something to face. This debt is not something we should run away from. I have to see what he wants. I won't mention your loan, but we can't pretend it doesn't exist either. Perhaps we can come up with some sort of agreement. But next time don't make any deals like this without telling me. Understood?"

"I promise."

"We don't do a thing without a deposit."

"I know. I know."

"No more sob stories."

"I didn't think it was a sob story," her father said annoyed. "I honestly told you what happened."

"Not yours, the clients. I'm saying you shouldn't fall for them."

"I won't. I've learned my lesson."

She wasn't completely sure her father had learned a lesson, but, like always, she would be the one paying for it. How, she had no idea.

But she wouldn't think of it now. She had to think of what to do.

CHAPTER ELEVEN

"You have to tell your sister."

Julia looked across at her best friend Chloe Schwartz as they sat in Julia's living room finishing off a thin crust pizza loaded with mozzarella cheese. Chloe's real name was Camille but she renamed herself in freshman year of high school because she felt Chloe suited her better. Julia agreed. Her friend was short with a nose so small and eyes so big she reminded her of a Kewpie doll.

But her words were as sharp as a crocodile's bite. Julia shook her head at her friend's suggestion. "No way, I can't do that."

"Why not?"

"Because then she'd be tempted to tell my mother who would then have to call me and tell me how much she thinks Dad is a loser."

"Which he is."

Julia frowned. "He is not a loser."

Chloe rested a hand over her heart. "I'm being as nice as I can. Lovable loser is the best I can think of. He'd be a complete failure if you didn't keep covering for him."

"I'm not covering."

Chloe rolled her eyes. "Oh, right, so you're *not* going to try to figure out a way to help your father pay off nearly a hundred thousand dollars in debt?"

Julia made a face. "Why did I ask you to come over again?"

"Because I am the voice of reason. The voice of sense. The voice of—"

"I called you to come over so I could ply you with pizza and try to convince you to let me borrow your beautiful silver jag."

"You cannot borrow Misty."

"Please. He cannot see the twenty year old junker I'm driving. It's all about appearances."

"No."

"Just—"

"Get a rental if it's that important to you. Or better yet use your Dad's Mustang."

"He needs it for another job."

"You might as well go there as yourself. If he doesn't like what you drive and won't hire you, then so be it. Better yet, he might have so much sympathy for you he may shave off a couple thousand from the loan."

Julia sighed defeated. She hated when Chloe made sense. "You're right."

"Of course I'm right." She took a sip of her soda then set the glass down and folded her arms. "Okay, spill it. How many this week?"

"How many what?"

Chloe narrowed her eyes. "You know what."

Julia sighed wanting to pretend she didn't. "I've cut down." She shifted her gaze and nibbled on the edge of a pizza slice. She knew what her friend wanted to know, but wasn't in the mood to tell her.

Chloe leaned forward. "How many?"

"Ten."

"You read ten books in one week?"

"I told you I've cut back. It's an improvement."

"You cut back from *fifteen*. You realize that's not normal, right?"

"Who wants to be normal?"

"I'm being serious."

"So am I. You'd be surprised. It's really easy to do if you don't watch TV."

"Or go out. Or date. Or—"

"I like my life the way it is. I am fine with it. I have no regrets."

Chloe looked at her doubtful. Julia hated when her friend gave her that look. It was a look that meant she was going to hit her with a question she didn't have a ready answer to. "Are you still afraid of getting a goldfish?"

Julia folded her arms. She knew she looked defensive, so she took a deep breath and let her arms fall at her sides. "I'm not afraid."

Chloe shifted her gaze to the far end of the room. "It's just a little eerie to keep a fully functioning aquarium with no fish in it."

"I like the bubbles."

"You do not need an aquarium for bubbles. Put fish in it."

"I killed the last one."

"Almost five years ago!"

Julia nodded solemn. "Do you know how heartbreaking it is to come home and see your pet floating on the surface? Eyes wide and accusatory? 'You killed me! You killed me!'"

"Fish die. It happens."

"It only lasted a month."

"Either get another fish or empty the tank. Make a choice. It's like you're stuck since your last—"

"Don't say it."

"Gallery showing."

"I don't want to talk about it."

"And it's gotten worse since your parents' divorce."

"I'm not stuck. Their divorce was inevitable and I'm glad they can both move on."

"What about you?"

"I'm adding to my portfolio."

"You haven't added anything to your website in two years."

"How do you know?"

"I've checked. There's this strange thing called the internet that makes it incredibly easy."

"I haven't had time."

"You have time to read. Have you taken any more pictures?"

She shrugged. She didn't want to admit that she'd taken pictures but hadn't uploaded them. "I got sidetracked."

"You haven't shown your work to anyone recently."

"I told you I'm not good enough."

"Just because—"

"I don't want to talk about it. I didn't call you here for that. My life is fine. Sure, I got a little sidetracked, but that's all."

"Yes, trying to help your father's business. You can't do it forever."

"I don't plan to. But you're right, I'll add some more pictures to my portfolio later." She wouldn't, but she wouldn't take her site down either. She didn't know why she kept it up when it was a reminder of her failure.

"So what's he like?"

"Who?"

"Mason Borden."

"I don't know. I didn't exactly meet him."

Chloe frowned. "But you got his card. You said he gave you his card."

"It was dark."

"Where was dark?"

"Where I met him."

Chloe widened her eyes. "*Where* exactly did you meet him?"

Julia laughed at the implication in her friend's tone. "It was nothing like that. I found myself in this room and it was dark so I couldn't see him clearly. He stayed out of sight so I didn't get a good look at him."

"Ooooh this sounds interesting."

"It's not. I don't even know why he wants to see me, but perhaps he wants to hire me for a...uh...secret wedding," she lied knowing that wasn't the reason, "and he's—"

"Willing to pay you highly for your discretion?"

Julia shrugged. "We'll see."

AFTER CHLOE LEFT, Julia cleaned up the plates, glasses and pizza box before she stared at the fish tank. She'd been telling herself that she'd get a new fish soon. However, soon never seemed to come but she wasn't ready to give up on the possibility yet either. She wasn't stuck. She just wasn't moving forward very fast either. Life hadn't turned out the way she'd hoped.

Her photography career had died a gruesome but necessary death, she was too busy to see anyone and after her last relationship, which also came on the heels of her crucified dream, she felt she was better alone. She liked her books and pictures.

They were plenty for her. That was what had been her saving grace with a father who couldn't manage to be an adult and a mother who loved her, but would likely have loved her more if Julia had been someone else.

A chance to go back to the castle was all that mattered.

A chance for something new.

CHAPTER TWELVE

She hadn't imagined it. The castle still took her breath away, even as a stretch of soot colored rain-clouds slowly parted above the building maintained a fairy tale feel. Julia parked her car still a little surprised she was there.

She'd checked her text twice and even had tried to call to confirm that Mason Borden was expecting her and that she hadn't made it up and had been met with a curt text that only said *Yes*.

She walked up to the large door and lifted her hand. Before she could knock it opened. Before she wondered if she were going to be met by a ghost or a speaking cande-labra from a Disney movie, a young woman in a crisp linen pant suit and short brunette hair opened the door and smiled at her. "Ms. Lester?"

"Yes."

"Follow me."

She was led to the main garden that had been

expertly landscaped to highlight the lush greenery. Her gaze landed on the purple chrysanthemums, her nose teased by the faint scent of lavender. "He would like to have you photograph the grounds for new pictures to put online and in marketing material."

That was all? That was why he'd had her come here? "He could have asked me that over the phone."

The young woman's bright smile dimmed. "You won't do it?"

"I didn't say that."

The woman held out a contract. "Tell me if this suits you."

Julia didn't see the words, she only saw the amount. More than she'd ever made before. If her father owed his mother money, did he want to take it out of her paycheck? Was that what this was about?

"You don't like it?" the young woman asked, studying the look of shock on Julia's face.

"I don't understand."

The woman's bright smile returned. "Yes, the Borden's can be very generous."

"Is there a way I can speak with him?"

The woman hesitated before she said, "One moment please." She disappeared inside the house then emerged a few moments later and said, "You can talk to him in the study."

Julia followed the woman down a dark hall with no windows and polished wood flooring into an equally dark study—but it wasn't an ordinary study.

It was a library with rows and rows of books and two floors with three ladders to climb to the vaulted ceiling. A large, arched window kept watch draped in the red finery of velvet curtains. They were partially closed, but not enough to keep a beam of sunlight from splashing bright rays on the maroon colored carpet. "He'll be here short-ly," the woman said. "Please take a seat. Would you like anything?"

"No, thank you."

But that was a lie. She briefly wanted to be left alone so she could explore the impressive room. Her heart quickened with joy when the assistant left giving her a chance to look around without being watched. The study was certainly a misnomer. Although the large desk near the curved window gave it the right air, it wasn't a stuffy place dedicated to academic work, it was too lived in.

She was surprised that she'd been allowed inside. Everywhere else in the castle on the Western side had a studied immaculate feel, but here she saw stacks of hard-back books near a chair and on the ground, a paperback on a side table.

They were not expertly laid out as showpieces but well read. The spine of the paperback had been so broken that it lay flat on the table like a butterfly with its wings outstretched. And its cover was just as beautiful with a pictorial image of some otherworldly planet. She smiled at the thought that the owner of the study was a science fiction fan. It was a contradiction to live in a house from the past and yet devoting time to tales about the future.

She picked up a book in a language she couldn't place and leafed through the well read pages and saw notes in the margins and strange doodles of an inquisitive mind.

She walked slowly around the room and ran her hand along the spine of the books as she'd once done as a child wishing she'd had the superpower to read any of them with the sweep of a hand and have the story or information memorized.

Her hand paused on a hardback spine with dark blue font on a light purple background. The title read: *Return to Love*. Intrigued that she'd found what looked like a romance novel in such a place she pulled the book from the shelf to investigate further and the book fell open to a page.

The words there captured her interest and within seconds she was transported to a love scene so tender yet sensual that she felt her body grow warm. The looks, the touches, the sensations made her feel less numb, books always made her feel less alone, but this one even more so. The two lovers were destined to part and she could feel their heartbreak as they were lying in each other's arms perhaps one last time...

"You can borrow it if you want," a deep voice said coming from above her.

Startled, Julia nearly dropped the book. She spun around and looked up but didn't see anyone. While the main level was bathed in the morning light the upper level was cast in a dark shadow.

"Where are you?"

"I'm right here."

She followed the voice and saw a black gloved hand gripping the wooden railing. "So you like to read?"

"Yes." She quickly and with some guilt shoved the book back into place.

"I said you could borrow it."

She hesitated. "Do they end up together?"

"It's a good story."

"But is it sad? Do they end up together?"

"No."

She shook her head. "Then I'm not interested."

"You prefer happy endings? I didn't take you for a romantic."

She heard no condescension in his tone, just a strange curiosity. "Only in my fiction. I don't like sad stories."

"Who says the story is sad?"

"They love each other and are forced to part, that sounds sad to me."

"The woman doesn't love him."

She paused. "Of course she does, the description of them together—"

"Is all in his head. Read it. You'll see what I mean."

"Does it end happily?"

"Define happily."

"Does he find someone else?"

"No, but it's a satisfying ending. He realizes self-delusion is one of life's greatest tragedies and true fulfillment comes from facing it. She could never have loved him. He was better off without her."

"But that's sad."

"Read it. You won't think so."

"No." She folded her arms. "Why is it called *Return to Love*?"

"You'll have to read it to find out."

"Or you could just tell me."

"Yes, I could."

When he didn't continue she realized the truth and sighed, "But you're not going to."

"You catch on quick," he said, amusement in his voice.

She shook her head and grabbed the book. She knew she wouldn't like it but was interested anyway. It wouldn't take her long to read. "I'll return it tomorrow."

"No rush. So, you wanted to talk to me about something?"

"Yes," she said getting her bearings. She'd come there to talk about the commission not about a tragic love story and she certainly hadn't intended to talk to a man in shadow. "I have a few questions. Do you want me to come up there?"

"No, I think we can hear each other very well where we are. What are your questions?"

She hesitated. It was rather awkward just talking to a voice. Why didn't he want her to see him?

"It would be better if we sat and talked."

"Better for you, but not for me. However, please feel free to sit down. Any chair will do. They're all comfortable. I can hear very well where I am."

She sighed. He wasn't going to make this easy for her. She looked to her side and saw an armchair. It was only after she'd taken a seat that she realized how enormous it was and it felt warm, as if it had recently been vacated. When she sat back, her feet couldn't reach the ground, the arm rests where the size of planks. What was the size of this man?

"Comfortable?"

She glanced at the three other chairs in the room

wondering if she'd have to pull a Goldilocks and test them out to find the one that suited her 'just right' then thought otherwise. She didn't want to have to stay longer than necessary. Plus, she didn't want to insult him. "Yes, thanks."

"Good."

"You know it's impossible to find a decent picture of you. They're either too far, your face obscured or blurred."

"I find photographs a nuisance. I've turned dodging them into an art form."

"I see. So where's the accent from?" she asked.

"Accent?"

"It's slight, but I can still hear it."

He paused before he said, "Long ago England. I left when I was ten. My father's family has been there for generations."

"Oh, that explains it."

"You don't sound surprised."

"That there are blacks in England? Of course not. They've been there since the time of the Romans."

"Few know that. My family doesn't go back quite that far, but about the 1800s."

"I see." Now came the hard part. "Speaking of family, I know my father owes your mother money."

She wasn't sure but felt she heard the tightening of leather as his grip increased around the railing. The tone of his voice seemed to grow a shade colder. "Is that so?"

She swallowed. "You didn't know?"

"I knew," he said in a quiet voice that gave her chills. "I didn't expect you to."

"My father has a hard time keeping things from me. I want to help."

"You'll be helping me a great deal if you decide to work for me."

"No, I mean with what he owes your mother. So you can understand my confusion. You can use anyone, why would you use me?"

"I like your work."

"I don't usually do commercial work."

"So you won't take the job?"

"I didn't say that."

He tapped an impatient finger on the railing. "No, right now you're not saying very much at all. What's the problem?"

"I'm trying to uncover your hidden agenda."

"Who says I have one?"

"The amount you're offering."

"Too much, too little? I need you to be specific."

"Is this a joke?"

"I don't joke about money."

"It's a lot. You must know that."

"Clearly I don't. I'm paying what I think the job and your skill are worth. I think it's fair."

She started to cross her legs then thought better of it and leaned forward instead. As large as the chair was it was oddly comfortable and she didn't want to make herself too at home. "Why would you be nice to someone whose father owes your mother money?"

"Again, that was not something you were supposed to find out."

"Why not?"

She heard him sigh and saw him withdraw his hand from the railing. "If you don't want the commission there's nothing more to say."

"What can I do?"

"Do?"

"If I took the photos, could you deduct the amount from my father's loan?"

She saw his hand reappear. "You'd want to do that?"

"Yes."

He tapped his forefinger on the railing again in a quick impatient manner. "He's very lucky to have you."

She smiled. "Thank you."

"I decline."

"What?"

"I'll only deduct half, the rest he has to come up with himself."

"But it's more than he can—"

"He doesn't have to repay the full amount, but he needs to make an effort."

"If I do the job for free—"

"I won't let you."

"What?"

"Here are your options. One, you take the job and accept the full amount. Or two, you take the job and accept half and I deduct the other half from your father's debt. Or three, you don't take the job."

"Or four, I do it for free and I'll do two wedding events if you want."

"No."

"You're being stubborn."

"And you're being naïve. I'm not an easy man to sway Ms. Lester. You decide."

"Fine, I'll take option two."

His tone softened. "Somehow I thought you'd say that."

CHAPTER THIRTEEN

"I hired a photographer," Mason said. He sat in his mother's living room. He'd stopped by to check on her hoping to find her in better spirits than she had been. She sat quietly sipping chai tea, her gaze lowered.

Emilia adjusted the bouquet of yellow roses and white and yellow daises Mason had brought with him. "What did you do that for?"

"I think the website needs it and the marketing materials could use an update."

"We had them done only two years ago."

"I think we need it done again."

Emilia shook her head. "There's no need. It's not like we need the business."

But Celeste wasn't listening to Emilia's complaints or reasoning as right as they were. Her ear strained to listen to Mason. There was something different about his tone. It didn't sound as distant and hollow.

She lifted her gaze to his face. There was something different about him. A new vigor to his features.

Something had changed him...or could it be some*one*?

"Who is this person?" she asked him.

"I've seen her work and it's good."

Celeste felt her heart quicken. *She.* Had this photographer caught his interest somehow?

"Doesn't matter how good she is," Emilia said. "We don't—"

"When is she coming?" Celeste interrupted her.

"Next week," Mason said.

"I'd like to meet her."

"I'm not sure that's a good idea."

"Why not?"

His gaze shifted to Emilia. "We'll talk about it later."

"We'll talk about it now. Emilia, leave us."

"It won't take long," Mason said, softening the request.

Emilia's curious gaze swept over them before she nodded then left the room.

Celeste clasped her hands together intrigued. "Tell me what's going on."

"Her name is Julia *Lester*."

"Oh, is that all?" Celeste said disappointed. If she was the daughter of such a foolish man there wasn't much hope for her. She had thought the couple's story a bit too embellished, but Emilia had persuaded her to give him and the attractive young couple a chance. He promised that he could vouch for them. It was only later that she discovered that he didn't know them and had been conned.

Believing him had been a mistake.

Letting Emilia tell Mason had been another one.

Mason quickly resolved the issue with all parties involved—the florists, catering crew, etc— and told her that when Lester was finally able to repay, he would handle things. She never expected to hear from that man again. She buried her disappointment. "What silly story does she have to share?"

Mason shook his head. "None. She wants to pay off his debt. She hadn't known about it."

Celeste stiffened, her interest renewed. "Tell me more about her."

"What is there to know?"

She took a sip of tea, wishing Mason wasn't so obtuse at times. "What is she like?"

He shrugged. "She's professional. I like her work."

She studied him over the rim of her tea cup. From the look on his face he seemed to like more than just her work. "That's nice but tell me about the woman."

He opened his mouth then closed it. He sighed and for a moment he looked sad. "No way."

"What?"

He sent her a knowing look. "Don't even think about it."

"Think about what?"

"This is not a romantic interest. I like her work, that's all. Full stop."

She didn't believe him. She didn't believe him because his voice sounded different, because his face softened just the tiniest amount when he mentioned 'her.' But she wouldn't push it. She'd made mistakes before.

Celeste set her tea cup down and feigned innocence. "I was just curious."

A tiny smile softened his hard mouth. "Of course you were." He looked around the room. "Is there anything else you need?"

To see you happy. "No."

He stood and kissed her on the cheek. "Then I'd better go."

Emilia reentered the room the moment the front door closed. Celeste wouldn't be surprised if she hadn't been listening by the door in the other room.

"Were you able to talk some sense into him?" she asked.

"I want you to leave this one alone."

Emilia looked at her surprised. "What?"

"You heard me. I trust his instincts. If he wants new photos he's going to get them."

Emilia sniffed amused. "You spoil him."

Celeste lifted her tea and said in a grave voice, "Not nearly enough."

CHAPTER FOURTEEN

"You still have that there?"

A surprise visit from her sister could be either a blessing or a curse. Julia hadn't been sure whether to smile or groan when she saw her sister standing outside her apartment door. She looked stylish, as usual, in a light blue suit and pearl earrings.

Julia didn't ask why her sister was there. It wouldn't take long to find out. She opened the door and let her sister follow her inside. She had hoped to return home and start reading the book burning a hole in her bag and then decide what she planned to photograph at the castle first, but that would have to wait.

"I still have what, where?" Julia said putting her camera bag down.

Her sister pointed to the aquarium. "That."

Julia rolled her eyes and sighed. "What is everyone's obsession with my fish tank?"

"Because it's strange to have an empty fish tank in your living room."

"It's not empty. It's filled with water."

"And no fish."

"I'll get around to it."

"How long has it been again? What did you even do with the fish?" She paused, narrowed her eyes. "Please tell me you don't still have the fish."

Julia looked away. "What did you come over for?"

"Please tell me that you flushed it or buried or swallowed it."

Julia stared at her outraged. "That's disgusting."

She shrugged. "People do it for dares."

"Mostly while drunk, right?"

"Sometimes."

Julia folded her arms. "Please tell me you didn't."

"We're not talking about me, we're talking about you. What did you do with the fish?"

"Nothing."

Myla pointed at her. "I know you, Julia. You don't do things the easy way." She studied her sister's face before her brows shot up in surprise. "Oh no."

"What?" Julia asked, trying to feign a look of innocence.

"You didn't freeze it, did you? Like you did when you found the dead bird when we were seven and you freaked Mom out?" She rushed to the freezer and dug through the frozen items before she pulled out a small sandwich bag with a frozen goldfish inside. "This is just sad."

"I know. I don't know if I overfed it, was the room the wrong temperature, was it diseased?"

Her sister shook her head in pity. "Not the fish. The fact that you kept it."

"I need to find out what happened."

"It died. There's nothing more you need to know. Throw it away."

"I will."

"No, you won't so I'll do it for you."

Julia snatched the bag from her. "No."

Myla quickly snatched it back, took out the frozen fish and tossed it down the garbage disposal.

Julia held up her hands. "Please don't—"

But it was too late. Myla turned the disposal on, filling the kitchen with the sound of a roaring engine and chopping blades. "Now it's gone."

Julia turned the disposal off. "That was just mean."

Myla shrugged unrepentant. "It's for your own good."

Julia folded her arms. "You could have done it with more dignity."

Myla turned to the sink and gave a mock salute. "Rest in pieces."

Julia frowned. "That is not funny."

"I know. You really need to move on."

Julia left the kitchen and sat on her couch. "Why are you here?"

Myla took a seat in front of her. "How did the wedding go?"

"Fine. The couple was happy. You didn't have to come by to ask me that."

She bit her lip. Julia felt her mood dim, that wasn't a

good sign. "You're right," her sister said. "We've got a situation."

"What?"

"Mom's getting married."

"What? I just spoke to her a few days ago and she didn't say anything."

"The proposal only happened two days ago."

"And she wants me to take the pictures?"

"No, silly, she wants you to break the news to Dad."

Julia rested her head back and closed her eyes. This news was almost as bad as her father's huge debt. "Do I have to?"

"I could tell him, but it's better coming from you."

It was true, but she didn't want it to be true. Myla had little patience for their father's panic attacks. Julia sat up and sent her sister a pleading look. "Can't she have a quiet ceremony and make sure he never finds out?" She snapped her fingers as another idea crossed her mind. "Better yet, does she have to get married? She could just live—"

"You know Mom is not going to do that."

Julia pulled on her lower lip. "Who is this guy? Have I met him?"

Myla cleared her throat. "Yes, twice."

Julia frowned. "I don't remember meeting anyone Mom's been serious about."

"It happened kind of suddenly. But he seems nice."

Julia leaned forward. She could always tell when her sister was hiding something from her. "What is it? What is it about this guy that you're not telling me?"

"It's Larry Brooks."

Julia fell back as if she'd been slapped. "She's marrying her divorce lawyer?"

Myla nodded.

Julia swore.

"Which is why I'm here."

"Dad is going to have a conniption."

Myla nodded again. "We can tell him together if you want."

Julia covered her eyes and groaned. That wouldn't help. "When's the wedding?"

"In about three months."

Julia's stared at her sister. "What?"

"It will be a simple ceremony."

"Mom doesn't know how to do simple."

"Just prepare Dad, okay?"

"Which will be so easy," Julia said her voice dripping with sarcasm. "Hey Dad, remember that shark you thought was the spawn of the devil? He's going to marry your ex-wife."

"There's no easy way to say it, just tell him the truth as soon as possible."

Julia's cell phone rang. She looked at the number and cringed.

"Who is it?"

"Dad."

"Great you can tell him now."

"I'm not telling him that kind of news over the phone."

"Well, at a least answer it and find out why he's calling."

She didn't need to answer. She already knew. He

wanted to know how her meeting at Wendhaven went. She didn't want her sister to know about it. "I'll talk to him later."

"Make sure—"

"Don't worry. I'll do my best."

Myla nodded then hesitated. "And...are you okay?"

"Why wouldn't I be?" Julia said, ignoring the panicked text with lots of exclamation marks that appeared on her phone.

"Mom finding someone and you—"

When another text came through, she turned her phone off. "I'm fine."

"You have an empty aquarium in your living room—"

"Filled with water."

"A frozen goldfish in your freezer—"

"Which you just pulverized."

"And too many books."

Julia shook her head in pity at her sister's ignorance. "You can never have too many books. Besides, if you think this is anything, you should see his library. It makes this place look like a doll house."

Myla's face lit with interest. "He who?"

Julia hesitated, realizing her mistake. "A-a former librarian."

Her sister stared at her for a long moment then started to smile. "No, he's not."

"How do you know?"

"Because of the way your face changed. Who is he?"

"It's more of a place than a person. The library at Wendhaven is incredible."

"But you said he."

"One of the people who work there showed me around."

"Books can't take the place of people."

"I know that."

"Don't let him win. What he said about your work is wrong—"

She didn't want to talk about her past. Especially *him*. No matter how long ago it had been the pain was still fresh. "I'll tell Dad. Now I have to get some work done."

"Do you need money?"

Not anymore. "We'll be fine."

"Don't be afraid to break out on your own. To do your own thing. Dad can't cling onto you forever."

Her own thing. Perhaps the job at Wendhaven was a secret she needed to keep.

CHAPTER FIFTEEN

The moment her sister left, Julia texted her father and told him things were fine. But a text wasn't enough for him and seconds later her cell phone rang.

"What does 'fine' mean?" he demanded. "What does he want?"

"The good news is that your loan is to be cut in half."

"What's the bad news?"

"I didn't say there was bad news."

"There's always bad news. Nobody says 'The good news is…' without also saying 'and the bad news is…'"

Julia switched the cell phone to her other ear and sighed. "There's no bad news."

"What does he want?"

"To hire me to take photographs of the property."

"Why you?"

She paused, surprised by his tone. "Why not me?"

"He doesn't even know you. Has he seen your work?"

"Yes."

"And he still wants to hire you?"

She took a deep breath. "Yes."

"I don't mean to be rude, it's just..." He paused and she could picture him searching for words. "Surprising. Your work is...different."

Something no one in her family could quite understand. "I can do traditional and commercial if necessary. I think I proved it this weekend."

"You did, honey. I'm sorry. It's just..."

"Unusual."

"A surprise," he clarified.

She could understand that. Her work wasn't one that many people understood, but somehow she wanted the chance to take pictures again even if it wasn't her usual style. She wanted to go back to Wendhaven and capture its many beautiful aspects in an entirely new way. She wanted to be a photographer again even if for a little while before she put her camera away again for good.

"Be careful," her father continued. "Don't be too experimental. They are—"

"Don't worry. I won't embarrass you. You're welcome by the way."

"For what?"

"The debt."

"Oh, yes, right. Thanks."

He didn't sound as enthused as she'd hoped he'd be. She thought reducing his debt by half was a major accomplishment, but he treated it as nothing. She pushed down her hurt and kept her voice light. "Let me take you to lunch Monday."

"Just tell me the bad news."

"Dad, I don't have bad news." Which was a complete lie. She had to tell him about her mother's wedding eventually.

"I can sense you're hiding something from me."

"I'll talk to you on Monday. Gotta go."

She disconnected. She didn't care that he was anxious. It had become a pattern with him. Waiting a couple of days would do him good.

She went to her bag and pulled out *Return to Love*.

She felt strangely honored that he'd let her borrow it.

But she ended up tossing the book aside twice (resisting the urge to throw it across the room). She was determined not to finish it, but somehow it kept pulling her back. And when she finally reached the end she was in tears. The story was terribly sad. But also galvanizing. She thought of her former photography teacher and the man she'd once thought was The One and cringed. She'd been fooled too. But she'd been frozen, like the fish she'd kept in her freezer, like the man in the book who became numb to life and distanced himself from the world as he moved through it. He accepted loneliness as the natural state for those who wanted too much.

But she didn't want to end up like that. As much as the thought of working at Wendhaven scared her it was a step in the right direction.

She didn't feel guilty not telling her sister or father the entire truth. She needed to hold something back. She was keeping something for herself. Everyone thought they knew everything about her. This was a chance to prove them wrong.

HEAVEN. She'd never imagined it would be so heavenly. When she'd arrived to take photographs she'd expected to be met with strict instructions, instead she was told the locations they wanted shot and that was it. She did the required shots of the castle, the magnificent entryway and corridors, Great Hall, main garden, and the court-yard before she dashed to her favorite location: The garden near the stone cottage.

She captured the sight of the butterflies and the wild-flowers, the sun on the stone path.

She took a snap of a bumble bee then stopped when she heard a soft growl.

CHAPTER SIXTEEN

It wasn't a menacing sound but it was something that caught her attention because it wasn't the kind of sound she'd thought she'd hear while in the middle of a rose scented pathway.

Deep in a dark forest, sure; alone on a cold mountaintop, yes, but among the bright blooms of flowers? No.

Julia carefully turned her head to see if she could see the source of the sound. Had some feral animal gotten lost?

Should she care?

She should just get back on the path and leave, be safe, but something made her move forward when she heard the sound again. It wasn't an angry sound. It sounded like a creature in pain. A wounded animal. She couldn't walk away from that.

She crept forward and paused when she saw the massive bare back of a man dressed in old jeans and sneakers, kneeling on the ground. She'd never seen a back that wide, brown and muscular before. And kneeling, he seemed to almost be as tall as her. She couldn't imagine what he must be like standing. He could probably pass 6'8.

She froze. Perhaps he was already tending to the animal. She didn't want to disturb him. She probably shouldn't be this far into the path anyway. When she heard him softly swear and make a strange sound, she peered closer and saw drops of blood next to him then noticed him cradling something. She hurried forward.

"Are you okay?"

He jerked, startled then he swung his head to her and pinned her with a glare that trapped a scream in her throat.

Screaming would be dangerous. He wasn't the kind of man who would take a scream well, although his piercing dark eyes and fierce features ignited the urge. If he hadn't been cradling his hand and she hadn't seen the blood on the ground, she would have hurried away. He wasn't the kind of man who looked like he needed anyone. Especially her.

"Yes, I'm fine." His words were softly spoken and not as fierce as the look on his face.

He was clearly lying. Blood soaked through the orange T-shirt wrapped around his hand.

She didn't know whether it was the voice or the blood but something about him made her fear of him disappear. He needed help, that was all that mattered.

"No, you're not. Let me see."

"No." He stood to his feet. Too fast. He stumbled back. She grabbed him and awkwardly let him lean on her but he was too big for her to balance and they both landed on the ground—hard.

"You're not allowed to faint. I can't carry you."

"I didn't faint."

Every time he spoke he sent shivers over her skin, his deep voice resonating within her.

"But you were dizzy from loss of blood, right?"

"It's just a little cut. The days' hot."

She looked at his forehead and saw beads of sweat. He was going into shock. That wasn't a good sign, right? She pulled out her phone.

"What are you doing?" he demanded.

"Calling an ambulance."

"I don't need an ambulance."

"You can hardly walk."

He closed his eyes. "I just need a few minutes."

"No." She patted his face. "Look at me."

He glared at her. She didn't care. "You need someone to look—"

She stopped when he shifted his body and pulled out his cell phone. "I h—have—"

"Shh, don't talk."

"I have a physician." He held out the phone to her. She heard it dialing someone and put it to her ear.

"Hey Big M," a bright female voice answered. "What's up?"

"Um," Julia said, feeling awkward. She didn't know that a gardener could afford to have a doctor on call. Perhaps he had an underlying medical condition. "I don't know why he called you, but he needs a doctor fast."

"Who's this?"

"I found him in the garden at the house. He cut his hand somehow and he doesn't look good."

"I'll be right there."

"He won't let me call an ambulance—"

"It's a tiny cut," he said.

"But I really think I should call one."

"Tell her it's a tiny cut," he repeated.

"No."

"What was that?" the woman said.

"Nothing. I just—"

"Don't worry," she said in a calm, controlled voice. "I'm less than five minutes away."

Julia hung up then asked him, "What's your name?"

"Doesn't matter."

"Of course it matters. I can't call you 'hey you'."

"I don't care."

She patted his cheek again.

His eyes flashed. "Stop that."

"Then stop closing your eyes. It's dangerous."

"It's the sun. Hurts my eyes."

Julia held up her hand to shield his gaze. "Okay, I don't like waiting like this but your doctor says she's on her way. Are you afraid of the cost? We can find a way to pay it down. You could lose your hand or your life. I don't think it's worth it."

"I'll be fine. It's nothing. Sorry about this."

For some reason she found his apology endearing. "It's not like you did it on purpose."

He glanced at her top and suddenly looked ill. "I even got it on you."

She looked at the blood on her yellow blouse. "That's okay."

"I can pay you back," he said in a hoarse voice. "Send me the bill."

"Don't worry about it." She touched his forehead. "Don't worry about anything, just stay with me." She pulled out some water from her bag. "Drink this."

He shook his head. "I couldn't."

"But you should."

"No."

"Just a few drops."

"No."

She sighed. "So stubborn." She glanced at her watch. "It feels like she's taking forever. If she doesn't come soon, I'm calling an ambulance."

"No you're not." He gripped her arm, not enough to hurt, but enough to get his message across. "Promise me."

"I promise," she said surprised by how adamant he was, suddenly unnerved by his size and strength. He may be in a weakened state, but with enough adrenaline he could easily overpower her. She didn't want to upset him. She looked around for a distraction. "You should have better supplies as a gardener. You should have better shade for your head, and stay as hydrated as possible. Is this a new job for you?"

He shook his head. "No I—"

"Okay, idiot," a female voice said amused. Julia turned and saw an attractive dark skinned woman, with hair sprouting from a misshaped braid, wearing stylish glasses and carrying an emergency kit. She wore blue jeans and a peach blouse that looked casual but well tailored. "Have you gotten sick all over her yet?"

He groaned. "Shut up."

"He wouldn't let me call an ambulance," Julia said.

"That's because he's embarrassed."

Julia frowned confused. "There's nothing to be embarrassed about. Accidents happen."

The woman clicked her tongue and she opened the makeshift bandage. She gave a low whistle. "I should take pictures of this."

Julia pulled out her camera. "Do you need it for documentation?"

"No, I was joking. You're a photographer?"

"Yes. I was taking pictures of the wedding party and later got permission to take more pictures of the grounds and—"

"Relax, you're not in trouble. I was just curious." She turned to the man. "You're lucky. You don't need stitches." She lifted up the bloodied shirt.

His eyes rolled to the back of his head and then he passed out.

Julia patted his face alarmed. "What should we do?"

"You should stop doing that for one thing. It won't help."

"But—"

"He's fainted but he's fine."

"The loss of blood—"

"Minimal," the woman said in a dispassionate voice. "The cut is shallow. I'll clean it and patch him up."

"But he looks so bad."

"I've seen worse in war zones." She smiled. "Don't

worry. I wouldn't let him lose a limb in a flower garden. There's no possibility of that."

She watched the woman clean, disinfect then bandage up the wound. She was quick and clearly skilled.

"Are you finished?" he asked, making Julia jump. She hadn't realized he'd regained consciousness.

"Yes. You are to take things easy."

"Sure."

"Think you can make it back inside?"

"I'll just stay here a little longer."

"You can't. Let me call—"

"No."

Julia heard the panic in his voice and understood. Perhaps he was afraid he'd get fired. "I'll stay with him."

He sat up. "No."

Both women rushed towards him. "Be careful."

"You shouldn't move so fast," Julia said.

But he wasn't listening as he shakily rose to his feet. His eyes closed.

"You can go." He motioned to his doctor, but Julia sensed he was talking to her.

"You should thank her."

"Make her leave." He glared at the woman. "Now." But the force of his statement faded when he looked around, his gaze landing on the medical kit the blood-stained cotton balls and T-shirt. Then his gaze shifted to Julia's face. He softly swore before he crumbled to the ground, she caught him before he hit his head on the stone path.

"Stubborn man," the woman said.

"He wouldn't let me give him any liquids," Julia told her.

"You're lucky then. He's going to be all right."

"I'll stay with him until he recovers."

"You'll have to turn your shirt inside out."

"What?"

She rested her hands on her hips. "He's not sick, it's the blood. It's not something he'd want to admit to, but that's the reason."

"Oh." No wonder he didn't want an ambulance. The situation wasn't as dire as she'd thought.

The woman bit her lip suddenly looking guilty. "I probably shouldn't have said anything. Please don't—"

"I won't breathe a word. He should be fine in a few minutes, right?"

"Definitely, as long as we clear all the blood away."

"Okay."

"It will be better if we switch tops," the woman said. "I can go home and change."

Julia thought it was a sound idea, silently hoping the woman's blouse wouldn't fit too snugly, and had completely taken off her top when she saw the shocked expression of an elegant woman she'd seen before.

CHAPTER SEVENTEEN

Celeste Borden's pictures didn't do her justice. She was even more striking in person—pure beauty and elegance aged to near perfection in human form.

Julia felt her entire body grow hot.

"Aunty," the doctor said. "It's okay. I—"

Celeste held up a hand and silenced her before she pointed at Julia. "And you are?"

"Julia Lester," she said surprised that the man's doctor was related to this imposing woman. Did they keep her on hand to save costs? Was that why he knew her? "Your stepson hired me to take photographs. And that's what I was doing when I found your gardener hurt."

The doctor turned to her surprised. "Gardener? He's not—"

"That's fine," Celeste said, interrupting her with a sharp look. "Is he going to be okay?"

"Yes," the doctor said. "I—"

"I'm not asking you, I'm asking her." She shifted her gaze to Julia. "What do you think?"

She thought it was a strange question since she had a medical professional standing just a few yards away, but something about the older woman's gaze told her that her opinion mattered. "I agree with his doctor. He just needs a little rest. I tried to get him to drink, but he won't cause any trouble I'm sure. I'm going to stay with him."

Her gaze sharpened. "You don't mind?"

"No, it's a beautiful day," Julia said, wondering if she'd said something wrong. She didn't understand why the older woman watched her with such interest. Perhaps she thought she was neglecting her work. "I will make sure to send your stepson the photos once they're finished. You won't be disappointed."

She nodded. "Good. Please let me know when he comes to. Call me the moment he does."

"Okay."

She turned and said, "Tracy, follow me."

"But—"

"Now."

Tracy quickly packed up her things. "Remember about the blood."

"Don't worry," Julia said. "I won't let him see any."

"And—"

"Tracy!" Celeste called out to her.

She turned and waved. "Coming Aunty," she said before she looked at Julia again. "Thanks."

"I didn't really do anything," Julia said surprised by the emotion in the woman's tone.

She nudged the man with her shoe. "Idiot," she said with affection before she turned and rushed away.

"WHAT ARE YOU DOING?" Tracy asked her aunt once they were both inside. She rested her bag down in the foyer.

Celeste touched a hand to her mouth, perplexed. "I don't know." She'd come to the castle to meet the photographer who had captured Mason's interest. She hadn't anticipated this.

"She thinks he's the gardener."

Celeste couldn't stop a giggle. "Yes, isn't that wonderful?"

"How could that be wonderful?"

Because she wasn't afraid of him. Celeste couldn't help but notice how protective Julia was of him against her. She found it endearing. No one stood up for him. They never found a need to. She also noticed the tender way she cradled his head in her lap. How she made sure the sun didn't shine on him.

She took a seat in the private living room. "Is he really going to be okay?"

"Yes," Tracy said, taking a seat facing her. Although she always looked as if she'd just crawled out of bed, Celeste enjoyed her step-niece's company. She was one of the few people Mason could trust and who loved him unconditionally. "Mason saw the blood and you know what happens..."

Celeste frowned. "Oh dear."

"But she didn't seem to care."

Her heart lifted. "Truly?"

"Yes, that's why you saw her with her shirt off. We were switching clothes so when he wakes up he won't see the blood."

"Very considerate of her."

"We're going to have to explain her misconception." She grinned. "It is funny though."

Celeste shook her head. "I don't think it's funny at all."

"What do you think it is, then?"

Celeste folded her arms as a thought came to her. A thought that put a rare smile on her face. "I think it's an opportunity."

CHAPTER EIGHTEEN

Buzzing. He woke to the sound of buzzing.

Mason opened his eyes and wondered why he felt like a kid again. He hadn't been on his back in the middle of a garden since he was twelve. But here he was looking up at the brilliant array of colorful flowers and greenery that surrounded him, the fragrant scent of roses and wildflowers gently scented the breeze brushing his skin. There was the scent of soil and...he took another deep breath...potato chips.

Wait. Why did he smell potato chips? And why was he lying down in the first place?

He remembered being in his private garden near the cottage then trying a new trimmer, but not being as careful as he should have and cutting his hand and then he saw...

Mason swallowed. He couldn't think about the blood. Just the memory of it slowly oozing out made his head spin. He remembered that he quickly took off his shirt and wrapped it around his hand so that he couldn't see the blood, but it didn't seem to be enough. He swore and then...and then...

He heard a voice and saw someone.

Her.

Julia the photographer. She looked worried, but even that was hazy to him. He only remembered trying very hard not to embarrass himself and not pass out.

He didn't pass out, right? No, he made a phone call or she did. He remembered that. That meant he was conscious, Julia kept hitting his face, he hadn't liked that but it was good. Further proof that he had been conscious. He'd kept his grip. He'd maintained control.

He remembered Tracy coming and nagging him like she usually did then she...

He couldn't remember her leaving. Why couldn't he remember that? She must have. That was good. His cousin left and so did Julia and he decided to stay in the garden. That was why he was here.

Strange how the ground felt so soft though. He turned his head and saw the curve of someone's jean clad knee.

Wait...no...

That wasn't right. It didn't make sense.

Why was there a knee? Why was his head resting near it? Oh god was his head resting *on* someone's lap? When had that happened? He shot up, his mind racing, his heart pounding, humiliation making his skin burn.

Julia looked at him and screamed.

Mason held up his hands and kept his voice soft. "It's okay. I'm not going to hurt you," he said. Because of his size and his looks he'd had to learn to make people feel comfortable around him and he was desperate to make sure she didn't see him as a threat. He hadn't planned to let her see him at all, but he'd have to improvise. The fear in her gaze hurt, but he'd almost become numb to it. "You're safe. There's nothing to be scared of."

He leaned back. He knew he was too close to her, which was why he could smell the potato chips and the faintest scent of strawberries, that was probably scaring her too. He inched back ready to stand when she grabbed his arm.

"Are you sure you're all right?"

For a moment fear gripped him. What did she mean by that? Had he acted in a way that had worried her? His gaze shifted to her hand on his arm. And what was this? She was actually *touching* him. Nobody touched him. Nobody dared. People stayed away, people never got close to him.

Yet here she was with her hand gripping his arm. He was suddenly too aware of the feel of her fingers and warm palm against his skin. He lifted his stunned gaze to her eyes. She even looked at him. Looking at him with...with...it didn't look like fear. What was it? Concern?

He felt his heart race. He didn't want to care. He didn't want to notice how pretty she was—how a wisp of dark hair escaped her ponytail and brushed against her round cheek. He didn't want to notice her brown eyes and how tender their gaze seemed to be, or the shape of her full lips and how soft they looked. How kissable. He didn't want to notice how her peach colored shirt clung to her body and highlighted the sensual curve of her full chest, which made him think of ripe juicy fruit.

She wasn't supposed to be here.

He lowered his gaze. It wasn't concern in her eyes. It had to be something else. She had been frightened before, he was certain of it. Perhaps now she was pretending to be...

He mentally shook his head in frustration. He didn't know. All he knew was that he had to leave. He had to get away from her.

"I'm sorry I took up so much of your time," he said. "Just send me your extra hours, plus the dry cleaning bill and—"

"It's okay. I thought it was fun."

"Fun?"

She nodded. "Sitting in this beautiful spot and relaxing." She lowered her voice to a whisper, which he thought strange since they were alone. "It's okay. Your job is safe."

He frowned. "My job?"

She nodded again and raised her voice to a normal tone. "You can thank me later. I'll be back tomorrow to finish up more shots. I'm sure the owner will understand."

"But I'm—"

"Oops, I'd better call her since I said I would." She pulled out her cell phone. "Yes, he's awake. No, he doesn't seem to remember much. Okay. Just a minute." She put the phone on mute then said, "It's the owner. Don't worry, she's just worried about you." She handed the phone to him.

"What are you talking—?"

"Mason?" He could hear his mother say. "Don't say anything. She thinks you're the gardener."

He paused and sent Julia a curious glance. "Why would she think—?"

"Doesn't matter. Just play along. I'll explain later." Before he could ask more his stepmother disconnected.

He sighed. He was too tired to argue. It didn't matter what Julia thought. He had to get her to go home.

"Is it safe for you to drive?" she asked him.

He nodded to the pathway. "There's a little cottage where I can stay."

Her eyes widened. "You mean you live there? I thought it was just part of the scenery, I never thought it was fully functional." She bit her lip. "I know it's nosy, but I'm dying to peek inside."

He hesitated. "I'd rather you didn't."

She giggled. "For a moment there you sounded like some stuffy English lord." She made a face. "But you don't want to show me inside because it's messy, right? Fair enough. I'd hate a surprise visitor too. But I'm open to an invitation at any time."

Mason couldn't stop a smile. "I'll keep that in mind."

"Good."

He headed down the path then turned to her confused when she grabbed his elbow. She met his questioning look with a soft smile. "I'll walk you there."

"You don't have to." He shouldn't let her touch him. He should move away, he shouldn't let his skin remember every tiny pressure of her fingers against him.

"I'd hate for you to faint again."

"I won't faint."

"Fine. How about this? I don't want you to stumble and fall and hit your head, gash it and have blood everywhere."

His vision became blurry as he thought of the sight. Blood. Did she have to mention blood?

"Oh sorry," she said realizing her mistake.

He gritted his teeth and swore. She *knew*. She knew his secret shame. It was worse than he thought. He closed his eyes. He wouldn't think about blood. He wouldn't think about how close she was to him, how she didn't seem scared of him or embarrassed by him. She seemed oddly comfortable. And—

The whack of a stray branch took him out of his thoughts. He touched his stinging forehead and his fingers came back stained. His pulse quickened. It was dark...but it wasn't blood. Just dirt. He was safe.

"Are you okay?" Julia asked. "Why are you walking with your eyes closed?"

If he didn't say anything, she'd leave him alone. He was supposed to be the gardener for some strange reason. He'd be a gardener that didn't talk much.

Julia sent him an odd look. "Hold on a minute." She stopped and pulled something out of her bag and lifted it to his face.

Mason leaned back. "What are you doing?"

"You've got dirt all over your forehead."

"I can clean it myself." He reached for her rag.

She moved it behind her. "Or you can stand still and let me clean it for you."

He sighed and relented, bending forward so she could reach him.

It didn't take long, perhaps three or four quick wipes but it felt like forever. She was attentive, caring, kind. He wasn't used to it. He couldn't let himself get used to it.

Unfortunately, he liked her. He'd liked her since the first moment he saw her that night, the way she looked at the champagne glass. But now he liked her even more. He couldn't afford to. He couldn't afford to care about anyone. She felt pity for him. That was all. Unfortunately, he'd grown so needy for any kind of tenderness that even pity was like a caress. A woman's caress, soft voice, firm hand. All things he'd never had. Never would have.

His gazed briefly dipped to her chest, intrigued by how her top fit her so snugly.

She self-consciously tugged on it, before she said, "There you are," and put the rag away. She walked him the last several yards to the cottage then said, "Will you be working tomorrow?"

"Working?"

"Yes, I'd like to ask you some questions about the garden. I didn't get all the shots I wanted so..."

He hesitated. "I don't know."

She looked disappointed, which surprised him but the expression quickly changed to acceptance. "Okay. Take care."

He walked inside, closed the door and didn't look back. He wanted to forget the day had ever happened.

She had to go away. He had to get behind the walls of his life, the one he'd built to keep himself safe.

CHAPTER NINETEEN

Taking a picture of him hadn't been easy, but it had been worth it.

Julia looked at the picture of the sleeping man that filled up her computer screen. She rarely took pictures of people, but she couldn't resist taking a picture of him.

It would be almost an insult to call him handsome. There was a cruel masculinity carved into every aspect of his face. And yet she saw traces of beauty. His thin lips were perfectly fine, his dark brows, which looked menacing when he was awake, looked as soft as velvet when he was asleep. And then there was the rest of him.

He was a large man. The broadness of his chest and shoulders were awe inspiring. Raw, physical power exuded even in rest.

But she remembered how quickly he had tried to reassure her that he was safe. He had lovely brown eyes. They were truly a window into his soul and more expressive than she'd thought they'd be. She'd seen surprise, wariness, concern, gentleness all in one glance.

He had the eyes of a kindred spirit.

She liked his old sneakers that had worn treads. The jeans that were so faded that after a few more washes they'd likely disintegrate. He knew how to make a dollar stretch. She could relate. She liked how he offered to pay her dry cleaning bill, although she could sense that the idea embarrassed him. Probably wasn't in his budget.

She saw the cover of *Return to Love* and thought of the hero who'd accepted loneliness. She didn't want to do the same. She wanted to take a risk and reach out to someone. Someone who created a beautiful garden and got faint at the sight of blood.

The thought of his phobia made her smile. She was curious to know more about him. She liked knowing he was as flawed as she was.

She wanted to see him again.

Too bad she didn't know his name. She'd have to ask Mason for it and maybe get a number too.

They had clearly lost their minds.

Mason stared at his stepmother and cousin in shock as the three of them sat at a table in the cottage kitchen. It was covered in dust from disuse but nobody seemed to notice.

He loved them both. His stepmother and cousin were the most talented, smart women in his life. He never hesitated to ask their opinions on key issues, but this was ludicrous. "You want me to do what?"

"Pretend to be the gardener," Celeste said, smiling at him as if it was one of the cleverest things she'd ever thought of instead of the daftest. "Your name is Mark Barlow."

"Mark?"

"Yes, we thought it would be easier to keep the initials the same. The staff has been made aware of the situation." She placed a 2G flip phone on the table. "You're only to use cash and this phone. It's easier to hide incoming calls and fits your budget."

"It would just be for a week," Tracy said.

"Maybe two," Celeste added.

"I think it'd be fun."

Mason rubbed his forehead. "I don't understand."

"You said that Julia's coming back, right?" Tracy said.

"Yes, to take more pictures."

"So you have a chance to see her again."

"Why would I want to see her again?"

His stepmother and cousin shared a look before his cousin said, "Because you like her."

He felt his face grow hot, ashamed it had been that obvious. "So what?"

"I think she likes you too."

He threw his head back and laughed. Of course they were teasing him. Why had he taken them so seriously? "Okay, okay you got me. What woman would want a man who gets queasy at the sight of blood? Point taken." He smiled at them, but they didn't smile back. His smile slowly faded. "You're serious?"

They nodded.

"You think she likes me?"

They nodded again.

He stood, suddenly angry. He was angry at himself and for the flicker of hope they'd ignited in him. "And I think you both have taken this joke far enough."

Celeste sharpened her tone. "It's not a joke."

"At least hear us out."

"Please," Celeste said.

When his stepmother looked at him like that he had a

hard time resisting her. Mason sat down and folded his arms. "Go on."

"Too often people approach you differently when they realize who you are," she said.

"This is a chance to remove all that baggage," Tracy said. "You're just an ordinary man."

He rested his arm on the table. "I *am* ordinary."

"You're a multi-millionaire."

He shrugged. "Dime a dozen." He lifted his arm and noticed the bottom section covered in dust. He wiped it off.

"Most people aren't worth a couple hundred million."

He shrugged again. "Good investments, property holdings, inheritance and lucrative businesses."

Tracy frowned. "Stop doing that. It matters."

He sighed. "So I'm supposed to pretend I don't have a lot of money and that's supposed to do what?"

"Let her see the real you," Celeste said. She stood and opened a window allowing some air into the stuffy room.

"And stop you from flashing cash," Tracy added. "You always overspend when you're trying to impress someone. Especially a woman."

Mason frowned. "No, I don't."

"How much are you paying her for the photographs?"

He cleared his throat. "The standard rate."

"With an extra zero or two?"

"Her work is good."

Celeste returned to her seat. "Really?"

"Yes. Why? Don't you trust me?"

"It's a bad habit of yours to shower people with money to keep them close but also to keep them away," Tracy said when Celeste remained silent.

He leaned back and the chair creaked under his weight as he folded his arms. "Does that make any sense?"

"You got Kathleen an apartment, which she used to host two lovers."

"Thanks for the reminder," he said in a sour tone. "I'd forgotten."

"The business venture you backed for Gloria went up her nose."

"She's in rehab now."

"And all the gifts you got Emilia—" She stopped and winced and Mason guessed that his stepmother had likely kicked her under the table.

Mason shifted his gaze between them before he leaned forward. "I'm not an idiot. I know how women think and why they're with me. I give them what they want and for a couple of months I pretend to get what I want, which is why I stopped playing that game."

"You don't have to play it anymore."

"We're telling you not all women are like..." She bit her lip when her aunt kicked her again. "There's someone for everyone."

Mason shook his head. "I'm not lying and I'm not seeing her again."

"You're not even curious to find out if we're right?"

Yes, but I'm not taking that risk. "No."

"Because you're scared?"

"I'm not scared." *I'm terrified.*

"You're only thirty-six. It's too soon to give up on love."

He shook his head. "I'm not doing it."

"Bet you five thousand that she likes you."

He grinned. His cousin was a general practitioner without her own practice who used her skill working in remote areas and consulting with local non-profits. "You don't have five thousand to spare."

"Because I don't plan to lose."

"No. Besides there's no way to prove it."

"There is. Pretend to be a gardener and ask her out. If she says yes then I win."

"She could have a boyfriend."

"Then the bet ends. Go out with her and you can spend no more than fifty dollars."

His brows shot up. "Fifty dollars? That's impossible."

"That's the rule."

He shook his head. He knew it was a silly idea, but he could use it to his advantage. "If I do this both of you have to stay out of my personal life. Permanently." He held out his hand. "Agreed?"

Tracy shook his hand. "Agreed."

Celeste hesitated. "No, I can't help myself."

"Then I won't do it," Mason said.

Tracy nudged her with her elbow. "Come on Aunty, this is our chance to prove him wrong."

His stepmother's hesitation strangely made him nervous. He'd had a sneaking hope that Julia may like him a little and now he wasn't certain she did. Perhaps they were trying to make him feel good and get him out of his shell, from behind his wall.

She took his hand in both of hers. "If I agree, you not only have to ask her out, but if she says 'yes' you have to woo her for two weeks."

"What about the five thousand?"

"Forget the five thousand. This is what I want to agree to."

"Okay," he said wondering why her tone was so adamant. And when he said the words, he saw her smile and a sinking feeling entered his heart. Somehow he felt as if he'd given her exactly what she'd wanted.

Before he could say anything more his cell phone rang. When he saw the number he froze.

"Aren't you going to answer it?" Tracy said.

"It's nothing," Mason said prepared to put the phone away but his cousin grabbed it before he could.

"It's her!" she said with a grin. Her grin widened when she read the text. "And she wants the gardener's contact info."

Celeste took the phone. "Let me see that." She nodded satisfied.

"This is proof we were right." She stood and placed a kiss on his cheek, before she rested a hand on his shoulder with a grip strong enough to make him wince. "Now you have to ask her out." She picked up the 2G phone and held it in front of his face. "Mark."

CHAPTER TWENTY-ONE

He felt ridiculous. Although a spring breeze blew pass, cooling his skin, it still felt like it was on fire, burning with embarrassment. He hadn't given Julia Mark's contact information, telling her he'd have to speak to him first. Now it was the next day and he couldn't escape her.

He stood outside the cottage and looked down at the worn jeans and T-shirt he wore and sighed. Usually they made him feel comfortable when he was ready to work outside. He usually felt most himself when he was seeding, digging, planting or cutting, but today the clothes felt like a costume and being out in the garden made him feel like a fraud.

There was no way he was going to get away with this, but he wanted to get it over with as fast as possible.

It didn't take long to find her. He saw Julia in the main garden taking a picture of...he wasn't sure. She had the camera lens focused on the ground. He peered closer to see what had caught her attention and saw what looked like a white shoestring with one end unraveled. Certainly not something he would want on his marketing material, but he couldn't ask her about it without raising suspicions. Perhaps the shot was for a special project. It didn't matter. He needed to talk to her. Unfortunately, he didn't know the best way to approach so that she wouldn't be frightened. He cleared his throat.

She turned and he expected her eyes to widen, but instead she smiled. A smile that didn't just warm his heart, it made it burst into flames. He touched his forehead not surprised to feel a drop of sweat. Damn. She affected him more than he wanted her to. He had to get this over with quick.

"You look so much better," she said. "I'm so glad."

"Yes, thanks to you." He shoved his hands in his pockets. "Which is why I'd like to take you to lunch."

"No—"

The loud roar of an industrial mower coming to life at the hands of the landscaping crew drowned out the remainder of her words but he didn't need to hear them.

A feeling of relief washed over him, even sweeter than the breeze rustling the grass and leaves. It was over. He could go back inside and stay away from her.

He'd been turned down plenty of times before. Hearing the word 'No' was all he needed. Everything else that would follow was unnecessary. He knew all the reasons and excuses people liked to give him. *I'm busy. I'm moving. I have a sick relative.* The excuses would tumble quickly from their lips only changing when—or if —they found out his money or parentage. But she didn't know that and he wouldn't tell her. He could feel the beads of sweat on his forehead cooling and he ignored the brief piercing pain that touched him, annoyed that a tiny part of him hadn't wanted to be right.

A part of him, a foolish part, had wanted her to really have been interested in him and not only offering sympathy for the poor gardener who got squeamish at the sight of blood.

"Right," he said with a brief nod. "I understand. I'll leave you." He briefly glanced down and noticed the bright red body of a ladybug crawling along the shoe-string. He couldn't stop a smile, that would have caught her interest, but as much as he wanted to, he wouldn't ask her about it. He turned.

He was half way up the walk when he felt something tug on his shirt. He turned and saw Julia breathing hard.

"For a big guy you move fast," she said, bending forward, resting her hands on her knees. "I'm not able to move that fast with all my gear."

He looked down at the camera draped around her neck, its lens firmly in place and the large camera bag hanging over her shoulder. "What?"

She straightened. "Where are we going?"

He stared at her strangely transfixed by her bright brown eyes. "Going?"

"To lunch?" She hesitated before she jerked her thumb over her shoulder to indicate something behind her. "Or was that you just being polite?"

"No, no...I—" He swore, his mind going blank. She'd said *yes*? He hadn't prepared for that. He swore. But coming up with lunch shouldn't be hard. He pulled out his cell phone to alert the kitchen staff. They could have smoked salmon in the second dining room. Julia would like the view...

Except he was supposed to pretend to be a gardener. He put his cell phone away.

"It's okay," she said. "We don't have to."

"What?"

"You don't have to do what you don't want to. I didn't mind helping, you don't have to feel obligated any more than that."

He blinked. Why couldn't he make sense of her words? Why couldn't he seem to make sense of anything right now? "I'm sorry?"

She slowed her words and he noticed that the light that had been in her eyes had dimmed. "You don't really want to go out, do you? Your face is very expressive."

He rubbed the back of his neck, feeling his face burn. "That's not it, I do want to." He bit his lip. "I was certain I heard you say 'no.'"

The light returned to her eyes and her face brightened with a smile. "I said 'no problem' but I had to take a few more pictures of the ladybug first."

"Oh." He cleared his throat. "I'm also...I'm out of practice...uh...going out." At least that wasn't a complete lie.

Her smile widened. "Also not a problem. I'll choose the place and you'll pay."

He nodded. "I'm sorry but it has to be under a hundred."

She started to laugh. "Sure and I won't expect you to fly me in your private jet either." She nudged him with her elbow. "What kind of woman do you take me for? Who spends a hundred for lunch? You're funny."

He wasn't trying to be funny. He'd spent that and more for lunch.

"Don't worry," she said. "I understand being on a budget. You're going to love this place."

CHAPTER TWENTY-TWO

He had entered a minefield.

That's how Mason viewed most places—restaurants, theaters, concerts—since few were designed to accommodate his size.

Mason surveyed the dark wood interior of the restaurant, the dark blue and gold colored carpeting seeming to swallow the light that came from the row of windows that faced the parking lot, to see how best to proceed. The tables weren't too close together and the lights didn't hang too low, that was a plus. He followed the waitress and Julia wondering if he should mention that he couldn't sit behind anything bolted to the floor, but before he had a chance the waitress stopped in front of a booth with a low seat and high table. He did a quick calculation and realized that he would be able to fit without hitting his knees or cutting off his diaphragm.

One more bomb avoided. He lifted up the menu and it nearly fell apart in his hands. He wasn't used to flimsy paper menus and it was so worn that it nearly split in half when he opened it.

"Don't let the looks fool you, the food is great," Julia said. "Here." She took his menu and handed him hers.

Not that it was much of an improvement. The seam wasn't worn but the corner was missing.

What kind of place was this?

"Do you like pasta?" she asked him.

"What type?"

She paused and the look on her face made him realize his mistake. What gardener would care about the different pasta families? "I mean...yes."

The puzzled look left her face. "Then you should try their spaghetti."

He closed the menu with gratitude. He didn't want to look at it any longer. "Then that's what I'll have."

He didn't expect a huge bowl of pasta with a meatball the size of his fist.

Julia must have seen the surprise on his face because she giggled and said, "Aren't the portion's amazing?"

He could only nod.

She lowered her voice. "Any time you want a dollar to stretch until it screams, come here. They can really help make a budget stretch. When I was younger, my dad and I would come here all the time."

"Hmm." To his surprise the food actually tasted good, he'd expected a more processed flavor. But seasoned tomato sauce and firm spaghetti coated his tongue in a warm embrace.

"So how long have you had your business?"

"Ten years," he said without thinking. The food was

so good he was thinking about taking some home for his stepmother and Tracy to try.

"Then you shouldn't be so afraid of losing a contract. Anyone would understand."

Losing a contract? Oh right, he was supposed to work for his mother. "I just don't like to cause trouble." He stretched out his legs feeling suddenly uncomfortable. His leg brushed hers, he quickly withdrew them. "Oh, sorry."

"That's okay," she said in a soft voice, her brown eyes holding his. "I don't mind."

He'd left a minefield and entered an earthquake. She shook him like no one else. He was used to people being intimidated by him either by his looks, his size or reputation. Although he had removed the latter, he was surprised the other two didn't seem to bother her. And for some reason that terrified him. He had no barrier against her open smile and welcoming gaze.

"So why has it been a while?" she asked.

"A while?"

"Since you've gone out."

"Work."

She frowned. "It really keeps you that busy?"

"No, I also...had a bad breakup."

"I see."

But he didn't want to talk about himself. "Why were you taking a picture of a ladybug?"

"The same reason you planted wildflowers that attracted them."

Caught.

She knew. She knew the secret to the choices he'd made.

She knew him and there was no judgment in her gaze.

All tension eased. He had nothing to prove. He could be completely himself with her. She didn't care about his phobia or his bank account. Instead of feeling vulnerable and exposed that she seemed to understand him better than he did himself, he felt enthralled. He wasn't alone. There was someone who understood. The same feeling that had taken over him when she'd first mentioned his garden overtook him. Except this time he wasn't just shaken, he felt all the walls he'd built around his heart crumbling and he didn't care.

He was thirsty for this kind of connection, certain it would never happen again.

The conversation flowed freely and they talked about the garden, her photography and then anything else they could think of. Julia glanced at her watch and swore. When Mason looked down at his own watch he realized why. Three hours had past.

He didn't want it to end.

Too soon they were back at Wendhaven in front of the stone cottage now cast in the afternoon glow of the sun where Julia said she wanted to take a few more photos. He wasn't ready to part ways.

"That was fun," she said. "Want to do it again?"

He nodded. "How about dinner?"

"Sure."

"Tonight."

She started to laugh then paused when he didn't smile. "You're serious?"

He nodded again.

"Haven't you gotten enough of me?"

Mason shook his head, his voice low and smooth. "Not nearly enough."

CHAPTER TWENTY-THREE

Julia met his smoldering gaze and didn't know whether to jump him or run. He wanted to see her again.

Not next week.

Not tomorrow.

Tonight.

She wasn't busy tonight. She'd planned to pop something into the microwave before she buried herself in a book.

But this was real life.

Better than any scene she'd read.

Here was a man who excited her with his steady, dark gaze.

Who also made her feel as if no one else existed. That they were the only two people in the world. She'd never been the object of someone's attention like this before.

"I have to take some more pictures before I go. I don't think they'll want me coming back a third day."

"They won't mind," he said with a certainty that surprised her.

"How do you know that?"

He hesitated before he said, "As long as you stay out of their way and do a good job, they're fine."

"You know them well."

He shrugged. "Well enough."

She bit her lip. It was reckless. It wasn't something she'd ever done before. What if dinner didn't flow as smoothly as lunch?

What if...

His eyes clung to hers. "Don't talk yourself out of it," he said in a deep, velvet whisper.

His words filled her with a mixture of emotions—excitement, fear, confusion—that made her shiver inside. How did he know her so well when they'd only just met? Why did his penetrating gaze make her trust him? How was he able to make the attraction they both felt seem wonderful instead of scary? She was so used to being cautious and scared. But since being in the garden the other day, thoughts of fear seemed to keep disappearing. She released a shaky breath. She'd come this far, she wouldn't turn back now. "Fine. Dinner but no dessert."

The corner of his mouth kicked up in a sexy grin. "I'll have to work on that."

He wouldn't have to work very hard. That night they shared a kiss that not only tasted sweeter than any dessert she'd ever tasted, but also faintly made her think of sharing breakfast. But she stopped herself before she took things too far.

Mason dropped her home that night and Julia made

sure not to invite him inside before she got out of his black BMW. She was still touched that he'd begged a friend to let him borrow his car for the night.

She stepped out of the car and waved. "Bye."

He jumped out of the car and looked at her over the hood. "Do you like the beach? I have a hou—uh..." He sighed looking dejected. "Never mind."

"What is it?"

He rubbed his forehead. "It's nothing."

"I do like the beach."

He shoved his hands in his pockets, lowered his gaze and nodded. "Me too."

"What did you want to ask me?"

"I can't give you much, but—"

She smiled sensing his fear. "That's okay. I like being with you."

His lifted his gaze. He rested both hands on the hood of the car and took a deep breath as if gaining courage. "Me too. Would you like to go for a drive along the coast this Saturday?"

"I'd love it."

MASON JUMPED BACK in his car with a buoyant heart. Julia was everything he'd thought she would be and more. A drive along the coast was the cheapest thing he could think of. He'd almost told her about his beach house, but had to quickly think of something else. He felt so relieved that for a few seconds he thought his ears were ringing with joy before he realized it was his cell phone. He grinned when he saw Tracy's number and answered.

"Where are you?" she said.

"Why?"

"I've been trying to reach you."

"I was out."

"On a date?"

He sighed. "Yes. We went to dinner. I picked her up and she finds the most interesting places to eat. You should see the portions—"

"Hold on. You picked her up?"

"Yes. I thought it would be easier instead of—"

Tracy groaned. "You should have called me!"

"Why would I call you?"

"Which car did you drive?"

He cleared his throat. He'd already realized his mistake when Julia had asked him about it. He still remembered the pleasure and delight on her face as she sunk into the buttery soft leather seat. "I told her I was borrowing it."

"Which car?"

He tapped his finger on the dashboard. "The BMW."

"You idiot!"

"At least it wasn't the Tesla." He shook his head. "I'm not good at this. Maybe I should just tell her—"

"No, we agreed to two weeks. A couple more dates and then tell her the truth. It's not a terrible secret and when you explain, she'll understand, but be more careful. Did she believe you?"

"Yes, she said her friend wouldn't let her borrow her silver jag."

Tracey sighed relieved. "You got lucky."

"I know and I don't want to push my luck so—"

"You're having fun, aren't you?"

More than he had in years. "Hmm."

"Then seize this once in a lifetime opportunity."

He did.

He grabbed it with both hands. So much so that a deception that was supposed to last two weeks ended up lasting six.

CHAPTER TWENTY-FOUR

Tonight he'd tell her the truth.

Mason stood outside Julia's apartment door, wondering if he was about to make the biggest mistake of his life.

He'd never been inside before. He'd made it a rule to keep their private lives separate. She didn't come to his place or he to hers. Then she offered to cook him dinner.

He hadn't come up with a good excuse to refuse.

But when he entered her apartment, he wished he had.

It was one of the saddest apartments he'd ever been in. It didn't reflect her at all. He'd expected to see some of her pictures on the walls—painted a lackluster cream— but they remained bare except for a lone calendar with nature scenes. He noticed a lit aquarium with blue gravel and bright green plastic plants and a tiny treasure chest. Her couch sagged so much he was afraid that if he sat on it he'd end up on the floor. The space reflected a woman who guarded herself even in private. There was no hint of her personality. It was the room of someone protecting themselves. He knew it because he'd done it for years just not to this extreme.

She'd been hurt and he was lying to her.

He sighed at the sight of her small dining table where two lit red candles gently burned and the scent of buttery garlic bread, sitting in a chipped bowl, wafted towards him. She'd dressed in a form flattering black shift dress and wore tiny gold earrings in the shape of a star. He'd tell her the truth tonight and then he'd go out and buy her something ridiculously expensive.

She set a large bowl of minestrone soup in front of him.

It smelled delicious.

And tasted disgusting.

CHAPTER TWENTY-FIVE

He had two awful choices: swallow it and hope it didn't come back up again, or discreetly try to spit it out.

He had an iron gut, he could endure it. Even though it tasted like she'd gotten rotten vegetables and mixed them with red colored sewage. It was almost an art that someone could make something so awful. But she'd made it for him. He didn't want to hurt her any further. Mason briefly closed his eyes and gulped it down before he grabbed his glass of water and took a long swallow.

He set it down and focused on his plate.

He didn't dare look at her. There was no way he was he going to finish this meal. Maybe this was his punishment. He sat back and sighed prepared to upset her as gently as he could.

He wasn't prepared for Julia to take a sip of the soup, spit it out and start laughing. "This is gross!" She stared at him wide eyed. "I don't know what happened. I followed the recipe."

"I thought you said you were a good cook."

She covered her mouth in shame, but her eyes danced with humor. "I lied." She let her hand fall. "I was trying to impress you."

Mason cleared his throat. "Speaking of lying..."

She waved his words away. "I know. It was stupid. The truth is I really don't cook, never have. Dad always did it because I was always too busy working or going to school. You'd think with my figure I'd know the way around a kitchen."

"No, that's not..."

She pushed herself away from the table. "So dinner was a disaster. Let's have ice cream instead."

"Ice cream?"

"Yes, that's something I know how to make. I promise. You can help me."

"Homemade ice cream?"

She nodded. "You've never had it?"

"No."

"Then you're in for a treat." She took his hand and gave it a reassuring squeeze. "Trust me."

An hour later they sat on two cast aluminum chairs divided by a circular matching table out on her tiny balcony. Mason found the seating cramped, the evening air chilly with the faint smell of cigarette smoke from a neighbor's balcony, but was too busy enjoying the cookies and cream ice cream to care. He sighed with pleasure and relief as the creamy, sweet mixture melted on his tongue. "Ice cream for dinner. I could get used to this."

"What other flavor would you like?"

"I like chocolate."

"Then next time I'll make double chocolate ice cream just for you."

She put some ice cream on a graham cracker. "Oh, you have to try this." She held it out for him.

He hesitated.

"Come on, taste it." She grinned. "Why so shy? I'm trying to feed you. Haven't you had a girlfriend before?"

Not like you. He'd never been with a woman who made him feel so good to be alive. Who was so generous with her time and attention. Who looked at him as if he were an ordinary man. But of course to her, he was. He was just a gardener. He took a bite, but his tongue didn't register it. Instead his eyes swallowed her up. He could imagine covering her in ice cream and licking his way to her warm, brown flesh.

"What's wrong?" she asked.

"Wrong?"

"You just growled."

"Growled?"

She nodded. "Anytime you're frustrated by something you make this low growling sound."

"Oh, uh...it's nothing." He leaned forward and rested his arms on his legs, wishing his heart didn't feel like it was going to burst. He had to tell her the truth. "Listen, about you lying about dinner."

Julia stood and went to the railing. "I'm really sorry," she said in a quiet voice. "The truth is I was distracted. I've been keeping something from my father."

Mason stood next to her. "Me?"

A slow sexy grin touched her lips. "You're my special secret, but no, I don't feel guilty about not telling him about you yet." She glanced away and looked at the empty playground below. "My mother's remarrying and I haven't told him yet."

"Why not?"

"He won't take it well. She's marrying her divorce attorney."

"Ouch."

She turned to him and he saw the sadness in her eyes. "That might hurt but what will hurt more is the fact that it's really over between them. There's no going back."

He nodded before he looked through the glass balcony door into her apartment. "Why don't you have any of your pictures on the wall?"

She froze like a squirrel caught in the middle of the road with a car barreling towards it. Her fear and panic surprised him. He didn't dare speak or move, afraid she might run. Slowly he felt her steel herself before she took a deep breath and said, "I haven't gotten around to it."

He didn't know if it was the too high tone or the way her voice slightly shook that told him it was a lie. But he wouldn't pressure her. He would be patient. He changed the subject back to what she was comfortable talking about: her father.

"You should tell him. You don't want to lose his trust."

She released a heavy sigh. "I hope I didn't lose yours."

He rested a hand on the railing. "Actually—"

She pressed her finger over his lips. "Let's not talk

about it." She bit her lip, grabbed the front of his shirt and yanked on it. "Let me make it up to you."

He frowned and looked down when she tugged on his shirt again. "What are you doing?"

"Trying to pull you close and kiss you. You're as mobile as a mountain. It seemed easier in theory."

Mason covered her hand with his. He could hear her breathing, smell her strawberry-banana shampoo. In a moment he could have her in his arms, but it wasn't right if she didn't know the truth.

"You're doing it again," she said.

He kept his gaze lowered, aware that if he looked at her he may not be able to control him. "Again?"

"Making that growling sound." She lifted his chin. "What do you find so frustrating?"

"Nothing," he said in a hoarse whisper.

"You can't even look at me. Are you sure it isn't me?"

He kissed her. He told himself it was so that she would stop talking, so that he could get her out of his system. But he knew he could never get enough. He drew back and met her gaze. "Is your bed big enough for me?"

Her mouth widened with a smile. "Thought you'd never ask." She took his hand and led him down the hall. The moment she opened the door he softly swore. The bed was big enough. It swallowed up the room. But there was nothing much else. Her bedroom had the same sad look as the rest of her apartment but a little more so. He saw a tiny dresser with an open jewelry box that looked mostly empty. She'd told him about selling some items to pay off her father's debt, but she'd done more. She'd deprived herself. The open closet lay bare her meager selection of clothes. And yet her father had still made no attempt to contact them about the remainder of what he owed. The thought filled him with anger.

Julia followed his gaze and said embarrassed, "Oops, I forgot to close that." She rushed forward and closed the closet.

But he couldn't turn away. He couldn't move. He'd already seen too much. She needed him. She needed someone who didn't take from her. Someone she could depend on. Someone who made her see how desirable she was. Who made her feel that she didn't have to pretend to be someone she wasn't.

Even if that meant he had to pretend for a little while longer. He unbuttoned his shirt, the heat in his blood not only coursing with desire but pure lust. "Come here."

"What?"

"I said come here."

She hesitated then did. He took her by the shoulders and turned her around then grabbed the zipper of her black shift dress.

She glanced over her shoulder. "What are you—?"

"Stand still. Let me take off your silk gown."

"Gown?"

"Yes." He slowly lowered the zipper, the sound of the teeth unlatching heightening his hunger. But he wouldn't rush. He took a deep breath. "It's what you wore to dinner. Don't you like the penthouse suite I got for us?"

Julia quickly caught on to his role play and laughed.

Mason pressed his lips on the back of her neck in a gentle kiss. "Don't laugh."

She covered her mouth. "I'm sorry." She cleared her

throat and suppressed her amusement. "It's gorgeous."

He pushed the dress from her shoulders and let his gaze rove over her body. "So are you."

She laughed again.

"I said don't laugh."

She turned to him. "When you growl like that, I guess I won't." She rested a hand on his chest. "Mark—"

"I want you to enjoy this, Julia. You're surrounded by dozens of roses in crystal vases, chilled champagne and—"

She covered his mouth with her hand. "Mark stop." She leaned forward and placed her lips against his chest then followed it with the wet tip of her tongue. She looked up at him with a naughty grin. "Why would I need all those things when I have you?"

She didn't mean that, she couldn't mean that. She'd grown used to accepting less than she deserved. "But—"

She abruptly turned and unlatched her bra. "But I will enjoy this gorgeous suite." She climbed on the bed then tossed her bra aside. His fingers tingled with anticipation of cupping her breasts in his hands. "And this enormous four poster bed that has room for both of us."

She was wrong. There wasn't enough room. There wasn't enough room to hold the anger and desire swirling inside him. The truth and the lies. He wanted her. He wanted to feel her body wrapped around his. He'd suffer the consequences of this moment, but all that mattered now was her.

He closed the distance between them and covered her mouth with his. She tasted like sugar and cream. She felt like velvet.

He wanted her to know she wasn't alone. He wanted her to trust him in spite of his lie.

He wanted her completely.

Julia closed her eyes, achingly aware of how long she'd waited for this moment. To feel his bare flesh against hers. But it was even more powerful than she'd imagined.

She felt as if she'd fallen under the spell of a sorcerer. His hands swept over her body like he was casting a spell, the raw ecstasy of his kisses enchanting her.

Enchantment had to be the reason why when he touched her, she felt as if she'd been swept away to somewhere else. Somewhere far away from her drab apartment, somewhere as beautiful as Wendhaven. She could imagine the soft feel of the finest linen pressed against her skin, the scent of roses. But it wasn't only her surroundings that felt new. It was him.

Her hands hungrily explored every inch of his hard, magnificently large body, but he didn't feel as if he had the body of a gardener. She had a brief fissure of guilt thinking so, but couldn't help herself. He didn't touch her like a man who labored, but as a masterful lover—a powerful man who understood pleasure.

Pure explosive pleasure.

And claimed it. Demanded it.

He felt like a man who belonged in a penthouse suite or a castle or anywhere he wanted to be. So when he slid into the liquid heat between her thighs, she not only knew he belonged there, but that he was taking possession.

But the thought didn't frighten her. She waited for a fear that didn't come. Instead she surrendered to ecstasy.

It had been so long since she'd wanted to be in her body and not disappear and be somewhere else: Inside a book or behind a camera. For the first time she felt like she was worthy of attention. Of someone's gaze. He made her feel not just beautiful but precious and safe.

Julia sighed in satisfaction. She'd found the right man to let into her life. With him life was simple, safe, consistent. With him she felt the joy she'd lost. The joy she'd felt when her parents were still together and her sister lived with her. The joy that had been there before she'd had to worry about overdue bills or being her father's constant support.

Instead, she could be fully herself and trust that she had someone she could depend on. She didn't know why she'd lied to him about being able to cook, but something about him made her want him to open up to her more. She sensed he was holding himself back.

She wanted him to know that she was good for more than finding budget friendly restaurants and taking photographs. She didn't want to pry about his painful breakup but she sensed it was the reason he was cautious with her.

He was anything but cautious now. She didn't know what had shifted, but something had changed between them. Perhaps he felt she could be the same anchor she needed in him. With him her life wouldn't be shaken.

In a world that constantly threatened to overwhelm her, she'd finally found someone she could cling to.

CHAPTER TWENTY-SIX

Myla was rarely speechless.

She had gone to Julia's apartment to scold her. After a brief conversation with their father she knew that Julia still hadn't told him about their mother's upcoming wedding.

But all thoughts of their mother's remarriage, their father's cluelessness or Julia's procrastination left her the moment she entered her sister's apartment.

It was so changed, that if Julia hadn't opened the door for her, Myla would have sworn she was in the wrong place.

She slowly walked into the apartment unsure of what made it feel so different. The walls were the same cream color, but for some reason they seemed brighter and not as dull as she always remembered. And the couch, the one she wanted her sister to get rid of, didn't look quite as old and worn as it had seemed only several months ago.

There was still nothing on the wall, she hadn't added

windows, the blinds were the same. But something was different.

Myla searched the apartment and then finally found what it was.

Her sister had plants. Four beautiful plants.

She saw two large snake plants on either side of the front door, their large sword-shaped leaves jutting to the ceiling. They stood like two sentinels guarding a palace gate and seemed just as tall. She shifted her gaze to the couch and saw a lush spider plant sitting on the table beside it, its vibrancy giving the couch a new sheen and finally her gaze fell to the corner where she noticed a ZZ plant, sometimes called an eternity plant because it lasted so long. Its gently arching stems with deep green leaves looked so smooth and sturdy an untrained eye would think it was plastic.

Something had happened to her sister. Or rather someone. Julia would never have been able to select such easy to care for houseplants. Ones that could go weeks without watering and needed little light.

Myla felt a little annoyed that she hadn't thought of them herself. But someone else had. Someone else who clearly cared about Julia.

Someone who had taken the time to fill her lackluster apartment with spots of beauty. Someone who didn't just care but knew her, knew what she needed.

"Who did this?"

Julia looked at her sister surprised. "Did what?"

"The plants. Who gave them to you?"

Julia rested a hand on her hip. "How do you know I didn't buy them myself?"

Myla folded her arms. "Because I know you. Who are they?" She watched her sister's gaze fall to the ground, but knew there was little she could hide from her. Not only had the apartment changed, but her sister's face as well. There was a new color to her cheeks, a joy in her gaze when she looked at her. "You're in love."

Julia's gaze shot up.

Myla grinned in triumph. "Who is he?"

"Why did you come by?"

"To scold you about Dad."

"I plan to tell him—"

Myla waved her hands before she took a seat. "Right now I don't care. Tell me who he is. Why haven't you said anything?"

"It all seems to have happened so fast. We've barely known each other three months but..."

"You love him," Myla finished when her sister's words fell away.

"I like him a lot."

"Where did you meet? What does he do? Do you have a picture?"

"I met him at Wendhaven. He's a gardener and I don't have a photo because he really doesn't like his picture being taken. But I'm working on it."

Myla crossed her legs and swung her foot. "You're lying."

Julia sighed. "I'm not ready to show you a picture yet."

"Fair enough. Does Dad know about him?"

"Not yet."

Myla folded her arms. "So you're keeping two things

from him. You might as well get it over quick. It won't make it any easier as time goes by."

"I know. I've been trying to find the right time."

"There won't be a right time. You'll see him tomorrow, right?"

She nodded a little miserable.

"Tell him then. Early. It has to come from you."

She sighed. "I know. I'll tell him about Mom but not about Mark."

"Mark? Your boyfriend's name is Mark?"

She nodded. "Mark Barlow."

"Does he know about your photography?"

She looked suddenly shy. "He actually likes my work. I didn't think I'd find two such different men who did."

"Two?"

"Yes, Celeste Borden's stepson and Mark. He actually encouraged me to put some of my work on the wall." She lowered her gaze as if embarrassed.

But the expression made Myla's heart constrict. This man hadn't only brightened her sister's place, but he was also encouraging her to return to the one thing she'd given up. The one thing she had loved.

Myla frowned. "Don't look so guilty. You have a right to be happy."

But Myla knew their father wouldn't let Julia feel the same once he learned about their mother's remarriage. She didn't want to see the light in her sister's eyes dim. Her sister was slowly reengaging with life again, talking about her photography without pain and bitterness. Myla wanted to encourage her just as much as Mark had. "I could use your help."

Julia looked at her cautious, but curious. "How?"

"I need new photos for my portfolio. I have an event coming up and I'd like you to take some pictures. It's a huge gala, so be prepared."

"Are you sure you want me? You could—"

"If you're good enough for Wendhaven castle you're definitely good enough for me." She stood. "I'll give you three weeks."

"Three weeks for what?"

"To introduce me to your new man." Myla walked to the front door and opened it before she turned to her sister and said, "Otherwise, I'm going to track him down myself."

Emilia stared not sure what she was looking at.

For a moment she didn't recognize Mason. A face she'd known for years appeared to her like a stranger's.

Something was different.

Emilia watched Mason carefully place her four year old daughter in bed and felt her heart skip, her body warm. She could blame the coming summer heat, but the air conditioner kept any signs of a humid summer away.

But if it wasn't the heat, something else was toying with her mind because Mason looked different to her.

In profile he had a rigid, strong presence of a warrior god. A god that didn't need beauty to be alluring. The power of his presence was enough.

She saw that power now in every aspect of his body as he filled the green pastel colored room. That afternoon he'd agreed to pick up and look after Bonnie. It was her nanny's day off and Emilia hadn't been able to because she had an appointment she had to make. But when he'd arrived at her doorstep with a sleeping Bonnie cradled in his arms, a sense of longing—fierce and urgent—swept through her. Briefly she wanted to be in his arms, wanted to lean into and be cradled in his careless strength.

She'd never felt like that before.

But saw something different about him.

She still hadn't recovered from that first shock as he tenderly pulled the sheets up to Bonnie's chin. Then he turned to her and smiled.

He wasn't classically handsome, she realized now that he didn't need to be. When had his gaze looked so sexy? And that smile...

His smile always made her feel protected and secure, but tonight it also made her feel like a woman who'd been alone too long.

How could she have missed it? Mason was so good with Bonnie. He'd make a wonderful father. She had made a mistake all those years ago and seeing him now, as he gently tucked Bonnie's favorite bear next to her, she saw how much.

He was the right man for her. She had let him go, but she wouldn't make that mistake again.

Emilia lightly touched the blanket. "She should be yours."

She saw an expression of pain pass over his face and regretted her words. She hadn't meant to hurt him. But the expression quickly left. He shook his head. "But she's not." There was no anger in his voice only resignation.

"I know you want kids."

He walked out of the room.

She turned off the light and closed the door before she followed him into the hallway. "I made a mistake."

"I'm seeing someone."

That surprised her. He was never seeing anyone. She knew he still had feelings for her and there hadn't been anyone since... "You don't have to lie to me," she said, keeping her voice low in order not to wake Bonnie.

Mason folded his arms. "I'm not lying." He rested his hands on his hips. "I wanted to come over today to let you know that you can't depend on me like you use to. My schedule's changed."

A feeling that strangely felt like panic, slowly crawled over her skin. "You're really seeing someone?"

He nodded.

"Who is she? What's her name? What does she do? Your mother never said anything."

He shrugged.

He was being vague on purpose. She sniffed amused. "I don't believe you."

He shrugged again, turned and walked into the living room.

Anger ignited in her. It wasn't like him to turn his back on her, to tell her that he couldn't be there for her. She could still remember the feeling of his arms around her as she wept. "You promised to be my rock. That you'd be there if I needed you."

He slowly turned to her. A flash of annoyance darkened his gaze. "When you really need me let me know."

She felt jealousy roil within her. He'd never looked at her that way before. Who was this woman who could make him say those words to her, who could break through his wall?

Emilia took a deep breath. No, it was impossible. There was no one else. She didn't believe that he'd met someone else. There was no way his mother wouldn't have mentioned something.

He was trying to save face. He didn't want to appear pitiful.

But his face was different, he looked far from pitiful. He looked... she couldn't stop staring at him. Seeing what she'd once missed, the beautiful dark coloring of his skin; the kindness in his eyes, even his voice—deep and reassuring—caused a fissure of awareness to course through her. This wasn't the man she remembered from only a few weeks ago. There was a renewed life in him. "Who is she?" she asked, irritated that she cared.

"Good night." He kissed her lightly on the cheek. He always did that, but for the first time the touch of his lips made her skin burn, made her body grow hot and briefly —achingly—the scent of him engulfed her in a sensual embrace.

She watched him leave, gripping her hands into fists so that she wouldn't go after him. She'd let him go, but wouldn't make the same mistake twice. She had to be patient. She had to plan.

She wanted him back and she'd find a way to make it happen.

SHE SHOULD HAVE BEEN YOURS.

Mason stopped in the hallway outside Emilia's apartment and rested his forehead against the cool wall. He closed his eyes. Emilia still knew how to hurt him. She could hit his weak spots. He'd thought he'd gotten over the pain by now but he hadn't.

I know you want kids.

Yes, he did. He'd stopped letting himself dream about having a family. Stopped dreaming about ever having a woman who wanted to stand by his side.

Until Julia. Julia let him dream again. Julia let him feel as if he belonged in this world. That he wasn't an abnormality. She accepted him completely—his looks, his interests.

But she still didn't know everything about him. She still didn't know who he truly was and the longer he waited the worse it would be.

But he didn't want to go back to being alone.

He pushed himself from the wall, walked past the elevators and headed to the stairs. He wouldn't let Julia go. This weekend he'd treat her. He'd take her on a drive where she could photograph the scenery. He'd take her to an expensive restaurant before telling her the truth. He pulled out his cell phone ready to call her but stopped when he heard hurried footsteps in the hall.

He turned and saw Emilia rushing towards him. He looked at her alarmed. Was Bonnie okay? "What is it?"

"Are you attending the gala this weekend?"

He silently swore. The gala. *This* weekend. He'd forgotten about that. "Yes."

"Will *she* be there? I'd love a chance to meet her."

"No," Mason said and suddenly Emilia looked triumphant as if she'd confirmed something.

"It's not usually an event you attend alone," she said with a knowing grin as if she'd caught him in a lie. "But I'll be your date if you need one."

"I don't."

"Maybe I'll get to meet her next time?"

She didn't believe Julia was real and in a way she was right. Julia wasn't part of Mason's world. She didn't know anything about this part of his life. "Do you think because you don't want me no one else would?"

Her smile fell. "No, I didn't mean...I was just teasing."

He patted her on the shoulder. "Go home. You shouldn't leave Bonnie alone."

"Mason, I really wasn't—"

"And don't play games with me Emilia," he said in a soft warning, "Don't make another mistake you'll regret."

CHAPTER TWENTY-EIGHT

"Dad, I have to tell you something."

Julia had decided to treat him to lunch so they sat at his kitchen table with beans and rice and jerk chicken from a local restaurant.

It almost felt right that it was raining hard outside. They were trapped together and she had no excuse not to tell her father the truth.

He looked at her. "It's about your mother, isn't it? You always get that look on your face when it's about her."

"What look?"

"That look of dread. What has she accomplished this time? Realtor of the year? Bought a new car? A new house?"

"She's getting married."

Her father sat back and folded his arms. "Have you met him?"

Julia nodded. You have too, she wanted to say but wasn't ready yet.

He sneered. "Good looking and rich?"

"He's comfortable."

He stood. "It won't last."

"Dad, where are you going?" Julia asked when he headed out of the room. "I haven't finished—"

"I've heard enough."

She jumped up and grabbed his arm. "Dad, you have no appointments today. Sit down. Let me at least warn you—"

He yanked his arm free and covered his ears. "I don't care. It's her life. I don't want—"

Julia sighed, frustrated. "Dad."

He pinned her with a glare. "How long have you known?"

"About two months."

He shrugged. "Like I said, it won't last." He marched to the front door.

She followed him. "Where are you going?"

"For a walk."

"At least take an umbrella."

"I don't need one," he said before he stormed out into the pouring rain.

Julia grabbed an umbrella from the closet ready to go after him, but the warm downpour had already soaked his clothes. It was best to leave him alone. She replaced the umbrella in the closet, took out her cell phone and texted her sister. *I told him just now.*

How did he take it?

She watched his lone figure disappear around the corner. *As well as expected.*

At least he knows. Don't feel bad.

Too late. I already do.

Never mind. When you see the display I did for this weekend gala it will blow your mind.

Her sister was right. The floral display at the exclusive gala took her breath away. The soft, sweet fragrance of coral peonies, stood next to orange dahlias surrounded by lush green leaves in tall, extravagant glass eiffel tower vases as centerpieces on the white circular tables. Near the podium, delphiniums beautifully complemented hydrangeas.

Her sister had outdone herself. Julia's heart burst with pride as she photographed the flower arrangements her sister's company had designed and displayed for the charity gala to raise money for leukemia research. She could already imagine which shots would look great on her sister's newly designed website and any marketing material she developed.

She finally felt like her life was going right. Like every arrangement at the gala her life felt just as beautiful. She was rediscovering photography, her father's business was recovering and she had a man in her life she loved. Julia took all the pictures she could, wanting not only to capture moments but the feelings of hope, compassion and purpose as well.

She was backing up to take a picture of how the light from a chandelier sloped over the leaves of a bouquet at an exquisite angle when she bumped into someone.

She turned around and her apology died on her lips.

CHAPTER TWENTY-NINE

Julia!

Mason stared back at her, his heart pounding so hard he could only hear himself breathing. Not the sound of footsteps as people slowly filled the room, their voices mingling with that of the wait staff expertly making their way through the ballroom.

She wasn't supposed to see him like this, dressed in a three piece suit he couldn't explain away.

But instead of surprise an amused grin touched her lips. "Aren't you a bit overdressed to deliver flowers? I'll give you credit. You're not dressed like a gardener but a successful businessman. I'm certain you'll get a lot of new clients." She felt the cuff of his suit and gave a low whistle. "Who loaned you this suit? Looks like it cost as much as a car payment. Or maybe even the car itself." She smoothed down the lapel of his jacket. "You look amazing. A little terrifying, but amazing. I'm here taking pictures of my sister's work."

Mason could only nod. She didn't know yet and if he was clever he could get through this without her knowing. "Right, I'm here on business so—"

"I understand you don't want me in your way. I'm leaving soon anyway. I wanted to get here before most of the people arrived and it looks like it will get crowded soon."

"Mason," an associate said in a booming voice that belied his reed thin physique. "You're back from Cancun?"

"Yes," he replied as he heard Julia whisper, "Mason?"

"Tell you about it in a second," he said. At the same time Julia said, "Mason...Borden?"

He turned back to Julia and realized it was too late to retreat. Too late to salvage his lie.

Mason heard Julia's gasp of shock then watched her stunned gaze jump from his hands to his feet, to his suit before she lifted her gaze to his face and a flash of recognition came over her face as she put his two identities together.

Shock quickly turned to hurt.

He waited for hurt to turn to anger. He could deal with anger. He couldn't deal with causing her pain. It made his heart ache. But the anger he'd expected—needed, wanted—didn't come so he struggled to come up with the right words to explain everything, but his mind went blank. So he waited.

He waited for her to ask him why he was there or even what he was doing, but instead she stared at his chest. She stood stock still with a closed expression on her face before she said in a low voice, "It was all a lie?"

"No."

She touched her forehead with a trembling hand. "All this time." She briefly closed her eyes, pained. "What an idiot." She opened her eyes but didn't look at his face. "I should have known it was you. There were so many similarities: your size, your voice, your hands, even your slight accent but I ignored them because I thought..."

"Julia, listen."

She lifted her gaze to his face. "Was it out of boredom? Or curiosity? You wanted to find out what it was like slumming with the commoners?"

Mason shook his head, miserable. "It was nothing like that."

"Then were you just toying with me? Just like the book, was I fooling myself?"

"No, that's not it at all," he said desperate for her to believe him.

Another guest called out to him. "Hey Borden!"

Mason waved. "Hey, I'll meet with you in a minute."

"You should go," Julia said in a quiet voice. "Don't let me stop you."

He grabbed her arm before she could leave. "No, this is—"

"Slumming in the cottage with the wedding photographer. How you must have had fun stories to share with your friends."

"That's not—"

He felt someone pat him on the back. "Mason, it's been awhile. Let me—"

He turned to the friendly face and said, "In a minute.

Talk to you inside." The woman, who wore enough jewelry to make a thief drool, cast a curious glance at Julia before she nodded and left.

He opened his mouth to say something but his ringing cell phone cut him off. He looked at the number, said to her, "Hold on a minute," before he answered. "Yes. Hi. Right. Um...I've got to deal with a situation so I'll get back to you. Right. Right. Thanks." He put the cell phone away.

Julia shot him a glance and said in a tight voice. "Let me go and your 'situation' will disappear."

"I didn't mean it like that."

"Mason!"

He groaned before he turned, flashed a smile and waved. "Sorry can't talk now." He grabbed Julia's arm and headed down the hallway.

"You're a popular man."

Only when money's involved. He ignored the bitterness in her tone and led her to a quiet stairwell. Once they were inside he faced her.

"You are the best thing that's ever happened to me," he said in a hard broken whisper. "More than you know."

Julia folded her arms unmoved. "That's a nice line."

"I mean it. I shouldn't have deceived you for this long. I'm sorry." He gripped his hand into a fist. "I got greedy."

"Why did you have to deceive me at all?"

He sighed. "Because I wanted to see if you'd like me for me without...without knowing how much I was worth, what I owned, my background."

Julia lowered her gaze. When she spoke her voice

shook, "I thought you were safe. I thought I could trust you."

"You can trust me. I may not be who you thought I was, but one thing hasn't change. I want to be with you."

She closed her eyes, pain etched on her face. "You don't need to lie to me any longer."

"I'm not lying." Mason reached for her then stopped himself. "I'm sorry."

She opened her eyes and nodded. "Me too. I'm sorry I let myself believe." She bit her lip and shook her head. "Doesn't matter."

"Tell me what I have to do to make it up to you," he said desperate. "I don't want to lose you. What do you want, if it's in my power I'll get it for you—jewelry, clothes, a beach house, a car—"

Julia lowered her gaze once more and tapped the ground with the toe of her shoe. "You really mean that?"

"With all my heart."

She lifted her gaze. "Then buy me a goldfish," she said before she ran down the stairs.

CHAPTER THIRTY

A *goldfish?*

Why had she said that?

Julia aimed the lens of her camera at a group of people enjoying outdoor dining under a red umbrella before she shifted to a gold colored Mercedes sliding into a parking space. She took a picture of a dime left on the sidewalk, a flag waving in the breeze.

The early evening light was perfect.

Pictures. She had to take lots of pictures. Being behind a camera made her feel safe, distant. She didn't have to be part of the world. Just record it. If she focused on taking pictures she didn't have to feel anything. She wouldn't cry. She wouldn't need to cry.

All this time he'd been lying to her. Calling himself Mark. Pretending to be like her and it had all been a lie.

She took a picture of a series of yellow petals on the grass, perhaps lost from someone's bouquet or perhaps remnants from her sister's floral creations.

It had felt like such a perfect day.

She had been so proud. Her sister had triumphed.

But she had failed. Again.

They shared the same birthday, but not the same fortune.

Julia blinked away tears. She would survive this. She'd pack up her camera and...

She inwardly groaned. She'd left her camera bag behind and she didn't want to return and see him again. She couldn't. Not yet. She'd tell her sister to get it for her.

Julia headed to her car, feeling like every joint ached.

He'd offered her clothes, jewelry and a car and she'd said a goldfish? Why hadn't she asked for something expensive? But nothing made sense right now. Not him and certainly not how she felt. She wanted to believe him. She wanted to believe his reason for lying to her. But what if...

What if he was fooling her?

What if she was fooling herself? She'd done it before. Let herself believe what she'd wanted to and that hadn't ended well. She was the one who had gone after him. He must have found it amusing when she'd asked for the contact information of his non-existent gardener.

She was the one who thought that she wouldn't end up like the character in *Return to Love*. Everything she'd thought had been real had only been a fantasy.

But Mark—no Mason's eyes looked sincere and her heart responded to the emotion in his voice. So much so that for one wild moment she wanted to comfort him. To tell him that it was okay, that she believed him even though she wasn't sure she should. As angry, hurt and scared as she was she didn't want to lose him. How strange was that?

She reached her car then stopped. If she called her sister and asked for her help Myla would bombard her with questions. She could just imagine her sister saying, "What's wrong? You *never* forget your camera bag. Did something happen? Did you get a call from Dad?" No, Myla wasn't an option and she didn't want to inconvenience one of the hotel staff. She wouldn't run. She would get her things and leave.

Julia returned to the ballroom glad that it was busy enough she could move around unnoticed. Not that he would notice her. There was nothing remarkable about her to notice.

But she was wrong. The moment she grabbed the camera bag she'd left in the far corner of the room, she felt someone's gaze. Somehow she knew it was *his* gaze. Not someone who wanted to ask her what she was doing there, or someone wanting her to take their picture. The sensation felt too powerful to be casual, too possessive to belong to a stranger. She slowly glanced over her shoulder to see if she was right.

Two dark eyes closed the distance between them. Mason was the largest man in the room so he was hard to miss, but he shocked her that in the crush of people he'd managed to find her. Perhaps because she was the most casually dressed, maybe because she was loaded with camera gear, but he made her feel as if none of those were the reasons. His gaze caught and held her still because she mattered to him.

The heat of his gaze made no question of it.

It also pleaded for forgiveness. It begged her to understand.

But he made no move towards her. And for a moment she almost smiled to let him know that she did understand, but then the light bounced off of the gold filigree of a woman's earrings.

And she was taken back to her disastrous gallery opening. The one that had hosted the same elegantly attired people. She still had the red V-neck cocktail dress she'd worn and later buried under her bed. And she'd felt honored until she realized that most of the people had been paid to come, that she didn't belong.

Her gaze swept the glamorous room, her sister's extravagant success and then landed on the large man holding three people spellbound. She didn't belong here or with him. It wasn't safe.

She took a deep breath, gripped the strap of her camera bag until her palm burned and left the room. She'd been able to face him without falling apart.

She'd never fall apart again.

CHAPTER THIRTY-ONE

However, she nearly did when Mason turned up on her doorstep later that evening.

She'd fallen asleep on her couch, after sending her sister a text congratulating her on her beautiful floral arrangements and promising her pictures within a week, and then fielding a call from her mother who was annoyed that her father had left eight messages in her voicemail telling her she was making a mistake. Julia had to finally call her father and beg him to stop before convincing him that the woman who'd sent him an email and wanted to loan their business money wasn't a sound opportunity.

Once she hung up the phone with him and returned her sister's call (she wanted to hear Julia gush about her work) she replied to Chloe's text (she threatened to buy Julia ten neon tetra fish that were on sale if she didn't do something about her aquarium soon), Julia collapsed on the couch, emotionally exhausted only to be awakened by the sound of someone pounding on her door.

She jolted out of sleep, her heart constricted.

She knew it was him. No one else could make a door sound like it was about to cave in. She jumped up and rubbed her eyes ready to tell him to go away.

But the delight and hope on his face nearly shattered her completely.

"I got it for you," Mason said breathless as if he'd been running.

Julia looked at the tiny rectangular box in his hand. "What is this?"

"What you asked for." He held it out to her. "Open it."

"But I—"

He took her arm in a gentle but firm grip and led her to the couch. He placed the box in her hand. "Please."

"Mar-Mason." She shook her head in frustration. "I don't even know what to call you.

"You don't have to call me anything right now," he said in a soft voice that cooled her anger with its tenderness. He nodded towards the box. "Just open it."

Julia fell into the couch determined not to care what he'd given her. She looked at the box with studied disinterest. She hadn't received many gifts in her life and felt immune to them. His show of wealth wouldn't persuade her not to guard her heart. She pushed the lid back then bit back a gasp.

Inside, cradled on a soft blue velvet bed, lay a solid gold fish accented with three diamonds.

Mason sat in the chair facing her and said with eagerness, "I know you like red so I made the eye ruby."

She sighed and closed the box with a snap. "Ma-son, this isn't what I asked for."

He frowned. "Yes, you did. You asked for a gold fish."

Julia briefly closed her eyes not knowing whether to laugh or cry. "I asked for a *goldfish,* the little creature that swims in water."

He furrowed his brows. "Why would you ask for that?"

She gestured to her aquarium. "Didn't you ever wonder why I have a fish tank in my living room? I think you're the only person who's never asked."

"You seemed to like a minimalistic style. I always thought it was an art piece."

Julia rolled her eyes, annoyed that she understood his logic. "Of course you would."

Mason stood. "If you want a goldfish I'll get one for you. More than one." He took out his cell phone.

She held up her hand. "Stop."

"It won't take a minute. I can get them delivered."

"I said stop."

"Just let me—"

She jumped up and snatched the cell phone from him. "Is showing off your money supposed to impress me?"

"No, I—"

She set his cell phone down. "Then just stop and listen." She handed him the box. "Put it on."

He hesitated. "You want me to put it on?"

"Yes."

He chewed his lower lip. "Are you sure?"

It took her a moment to understand his hesitation. She fought the urge to shake him. "I mean put it on *me*."

His face brightened. "So you've forgiven me then?"

She waved the box at him. "No, I plan to keep your ridiculously expensive gift—"

"Actually, it's not that expensive."

"And throw you out."

Mason shoved his hands in his pockets and nodded. "And I'd deserve that."

"But I'm not going to."

He lowered his gaze as well as his voice. "Why not?"

I don't know. Julia opened the box again and stared down at the necklace. It was beautifully designed with each gill carefully carved. "Because being angry at you is hard." She shook her head amazed and bit back a laugh. "I can't believe you bought me this."

Mason took the necklace and fastened it around her neck before he placed a light kiss behind her ear. "I never meant to hurt you." His voice deepened. "Please believe that."

She swallowed and nodded too afraid to speak.

He wrapped his arms around her. "You're very special to me."

"Stop saying what I want to hear." She closed her eyes and took a deep breath. She wanted to run but she wouldn't. He still felt the same, sounded the same, smelled the same. She liked the feel of his arms around her, the warm solid breadth of his chest.

The connection she'd felt when she'd seen him in the garden hadn't gone away. But there still were so many questions. Still a part of him she didn't understand. She bit her lip. "Why didn't you let me see you the first time we met?"

"I didn't want to frighten you."

She sniffed. "Try again."

"I'm serious."

"But there's nothing frightening about you." When he fell silent she turned to him. "You're not."

"You say that now, but...if you'd seen me then you would have been intimidated. I know the affect I have on people."

She took a step back and let her gaze travel up his large frame. "You're right. I would have been nervous if I'd seen you like this."

"Exactly. You were scared. I saw your hands trembling."

"Because you were wearing black gloves like a serial killer."

He lifted a brow. "Or a motorcyclist."

"You ride a motorcycle?" she said surprised.

He shook his head. "No."

"Then why the gloves?"

He sighed and shifted his gaze. "It's embarrassing, but...I always wear them when I'm handling my dad's things. I'm always extra careful with his journals and writings. It was a sort of joke between us. When I was a kid I used to break things and he'd tell me to 'Mind out' 'Be careful.' So I started always coming into his office with gloves on as a reminder." He returned his gaze to her face. "I never stopped."

Julia smiled a little sad. "I wish you'd have given me a chance to prove you wrong. To prove that I would have been nervous but not frightened or scared." She lightly touched his cheek. "How could I be frightened of a man who owned a little budgie and read a sad book called *Return to Love*? But I'd never imagine he'd..." She let her hand fall and turned away.

"He'd what?"

"Look at me."

"Why wouldn't he look at you?"

Julia sent him a look. "Don't be naive."

"I'm not."

She folded her arms. "Right. A guy like you is really going to fall for some plain—"

"You're not plain."

"Struggling photographer who got lost in your castle and whose father—"

Mason gritted his teeth. "Leave your father out of it."

"Owes your family money."

"When you sent me the photographs, I knew I'd found an attractive talented woman I wanted to know better."

Julia let her hands fall to her hips. "Really?"

Mason shrugged. "Did you really think I needed new photos of the castle?"

"Would you have asked me out?"

He shook his head. "No, I would have watched you from afar."

"Like a stalker."

He grinned. "Somehow that doesn't sound quite as romantic."

"Because it's not. I would have preferred if you'd approached me. Think of all the time we missed."

"But we didn't miss anytime. I got to know you in the end."

Julia narrowed her eyes. "Through deceptive means."

He placed a kiss on her forehead. "I've already apologized for that."

She licked her lip. "Am I very different than her?"

"Her?"

"The one who broke your heart?"

Mason lowered his gaze. "Who said my heart was broken?"

"Your face when you said you had a bad break up. Or was that a lie too?"

He shook his head. "It wasn't a lie."

Julia folded her arms, feeling suddenly tense. "So am I different than her?"

"You're like no one I've ever dated before." He pulled her close. "That's what I like the best."

"That's going to make things complicated. You'll have to tell your mother about me."

He paused. "She already knows."

Julia blinked, surprised. "What?"

"To be honest this whole mess was her idea."

"What? Why?"

"You can ask her yourself."

"No. I don't want to." She pushed herself away from him. "Your family is strange."

"I know. Let me take you away. Let's try to start fresh. Where would you like me to take you?"

Julia rubbed her forehead. "I can hardly think right now. I don't care."

Mason grinned. "Let me find out if you mean that."

CHAPTER THIRTY-TWO

The last thing she expected was to be enchanted by the sight of thousands of various flamingos, their pink feathers extra brilliant against the electric blue waters of the Great Rift Valley in Kenya.

She also spotted rhinos, zebras, lions and buffalo.

She'd thought Mason had been joking when he'd told her to pack gloves and layered clothing for a one week safari in a country on the equator. But when they woke one chilly morning—after a nice warm mug of coffee and rusks (a dry biscuit that looked like large biscotti)—and they were packed into the open jeep, the moment she felt the wind sweep through, making the temperature feel as if it were 30 degrees Fahrenheit, she wished she'd packed a wooly hat and scarf as well.

But by the afternoon all that mattered were the abundant sights and sounds of the beauty around them from the rumbling of the jeep as it made its way along a dusty, bumpy road to the sight of an athletic dash of a herd of impalas.

At one breakfast, she watched in awe as Mason made his way through skyscraper high blueberry crumpets smothered in syrup. He later showed her how to eat the stiff white porridge called ugali, which was used for dipping into the savory stew of beans, onions, tomatoes and spices boiled together for dinner.

She almost got addicted to *biskuti ya nazi*—a coconut macaroon biscuit.

At the end of their East African safari, Mason took her on a two day retreat to a private, luxury beach house where they could swim in the warm waters of the Indian Ocean.

The day before they were to leave they sat on the patio and looked at the haze of a crimson, purple and lemon hued sunset. "Am I completely forgiven now?" he asked her.

Julia turned to him, the setting sun casting half of his face in shadow. In the distance she heard the cawing of a bird. The sound reminded her of the rumpled white linen sheets in the elegant tented room where she'd entered his arms without hesitation. She'd tasted rooibos tea on his lips, the feel of his warm breath against her neck, the touch of his bare flesh against hers. She'd been faintly aware of the soft cry of a bird then, but not like this. Not when his dark eyes searched hers, asking another question he didn't dare say with his mouth. *Do you trust me?*

She shifted her gaze unable to look at him, still

unable to handle how much he meant to her. How precious he was.

She heard him release a sigh and the sound was sad, dejected. She could imagine him searching his mind to find ways to prove himself more. Wondering if he should have taken her somewhere else. She didn't want him to question himself. He'd given her all she could have dreamed of and more.

She held out her hand. It was only seconds later she felt his large hand wrap around hers. "Yes," she said in a whisper.

He briefly tightened his hand around hers before she felt his soft lips kiss the back of her hand. "Thank you."

She kept her gaze fastened on the horizon, afraid that if she looked at him she'd start to weep. Her heart was so filled with joy it scared her a little. It was going to be okay. No more surprises. Over the past few days she had come to rediscover a man she knew she loved. She hadn't lost him.

"Before we head home, there's someone I want you to meet."

The words struck her with more force than they were probably meant to. But they sounded important. Too important. "Who?"

"It will be fine. Don't worry," Mason said with a smile.

Julia forced a smile of her own, trying to tap down her rising panic.

CHAPTER THIRTY-THREE

She'd had no interest in having afternoon high-tea in Kenya but once she was ushered into the large dining hall of an elegant north London flat Julia knew she likely couldn't avoid it. They sat in the eclectically styled dining room where an assortment of finger sandwiches and scones sat on a tiered cake stand.

She was too nervous to eat anything so let her gaze survey the elegant room.

She briefly let her gaze settle on a framed portrait in the corner. "Your father?"

Mason nodded. "My mother was a medical student from Ghana. They met and fell in love. I remember her giving me a long lecture on the dangers of smoking and me pretending not to know where she hid her cigarettes. An aneurysm took her when I was young. My father took care to try to be both mother and father to me. Even when he remarried he made sure that I didn't feel left out of his happiness. He was generous that way. He always wanted to ease someone's suffering, which was what hurt the most in the end because I could do little to ease his. I still miss him."

She rubbed his arm. "He sounds like an amazing person."

"He was," Tracy said. "He would have liked you."

Julia shifted her gaze to the third person in the room who was enjoying all the carefully displayed food the table had to offer.

She watched Tracy, a woman Julia now knew to be Mason's cousin and not just his doctor, spread a heavy dollop of clotted cream on a scone before she took a bite. Tracy said she happened to be in London for a conference, but Julia wasn't sure she believed her. She was friendly enough when she offered to take her shopping to make up for their family ruse, but Julia suspected there was something more to the innocent offer and kindly turned it down.

Mason handed his cousin a napkin when cream splattered her top. "You're a mess."

"I have to eat fast," Tracy said, dabbing at the stain. "Gran's in a mood. You probably should have come later in the year."

"Afraid it couldn't be helped. We won't be long."

Tracy shook her head. "Still not sure this is a good idea."

"Julia will have to meet her eventually."

Suddenly two loud voices speaking French resounded through the hall. "That's my cue." Tracy quickly finished her scone grabbed two finger sandwiches in her napkin and dashed out the door. "Au revoir."

Julia looked at Tracy's retreating back confused as the French voices grew closer. "I thought you said your family was English."

"We are, but Gran likes to get into her French season where she'll only speak it for months. We're lucky she's not in her Malay phase."

"Malay?"

"Yes, she's a polyglot. Speaks seven languages and thinks by focusing on them they will stay fresh in her mind. It's infuriating."

Before Julia could ask any more questions an imposing light-skinned black woman with sharp features entered the room. She wore a red silk blouse and black trousers, her silver shoulder-length hair swept back from her face with two large combs. Her keen dark gaze landed on Julia and gave her the shivers.

"Hello, Gran," Mason said kissing both cheeks. "This is Julia."

She looked at Julia, allowed the corner of her mouth to lift in the barest attempt at a smile before she said something to Mason.

He shook his head. "No, I will not speak French since Julia wouldn't be able to understand us."

His grandmother shrugged and sat before she asked him a series of questions.

"She's a photographer," he said. "We met at a wedding. Yes, Mum still hosts them."

She asked more questions one that so shocked him that he forgot his commitment to speak English. He replied in French his voice tense.

His grandmother lifted a finger sandwich and fired back.

His voice grew more adamant.

She took a bite of the sandwich and set it down before she waved her hand in Julia's direction and said something in a manner that Julia couldn't tell whether she was being insulted or complimented.

Mason leaned forward, his gaze fixed, his voice low. She couldn't tell much by his expression either. She thought she sensed some embarrassment, maybe annoyance and something else. In her rudimentary French she could pick out the words 'Gavin', 'seen', 'careful'.

Finally his grandmother clasped her hands together and laughed before she said, "How absolutely marvelous," in perfect English. She shifted her gaze to Julia. "Do you do portraits?"

"Not really," Julia said stunned by the woman's transformation. She didn't look as foreboding as she had only moments ago. Perhaps that was a trait Mason had inherited.

She stood. "I think the lighting is perfect in the lounge." She left before Julia could protest.

Julia looked at Mason confused. "Lounge?"

"It's the sitting—uh living room. You won't miss it."

Julia stood. "What did you say to her?"

He rubbed his forehead. "You don't want to keep her waiting."

She paused when she noticed he hadn't stood as well. "You're not coming too?"

He shook his head. "She wants to talk to you alone. Relax. It won't take long."

"But is something wrong?"

He winked. "Not at all."

JULIA ENTERED the lounge which was shockingly bright compared to the dining hall. The selection of plants, Julia expected; the orange couch and purple rug, not so much.

His grandmother sat in a large armchair with gold accent.

She motioned to a chair. "Please take a seat."

Julia didn't dare protest. "You have a lovely home."

"How kind," she said with false humility. Her dark gaze said, "Yes, I know. Clever of you to notice." She clasped her hands in her lap. "I want to trust you. I've been told I'm fairly good at reading people. The last one..." She shook her head, and scrunched her nose as if she'd smelled something foul. "Emilia was a mistake. I could have told Celeste to be careful there, but she wouldn't listen and neither would he. Poor Mason." She clicked her tongue in annoyance. "I should have handled it differently then, but I don't make the same mistake twice."

Her gaze lowered to Julia's necklace. "Did he give you that?"

Julia nervously toyed with the gold fish before she let her hand fall. "Yes."

"And the earrings too?"

"Yes, he bought them for me—"

"On one of your travels together? Don't look so surprised my dear. I know how my grandson thinks. He has a grotesquely irritating habit of spoiling whichever woman he's with. You'll be no different."

"But I'm not—"

"Like the others?" she interrupted shifting her gaze to the window. Her voice grew soft, pensive. "No, I can see that, which is somewhat refreshing. He needs a change, but I wonder if you're the right kind." She met Julia's eyes and held her gaze. "We both know he didn't win you over with his looks so what first caught your interest? His money or his status?"

"His garden."

His grandmother blinked. "I'm sorry?"

"The first thing I liked about Mason was his garden. No, I will not explain the reason why, the reason is private, but I will say that I like his face and I love his body."

His grandmother clapped her hands and smiled. "Well, you are unexpected." She leaned forward and her smile disappeared. "So I'll be brief. I've buried a son and seen a grandchild left heartbroken. I don't want to face that again.

"I will not stand and see Mason get hurt again. If you don't care about him, if you feel swayed to leave him walk away now. Because I will take my time to make your life a living hell if you decide to use him and toss him aside like she did. I will also make your family's life miserable. C'est compris?"

Julia nodded understanding her completely. She took a deep breath then replied with one of the few French words she remembered from school. "Parfaitement."

Emilia. Who was Emilia? She'd known Mason for three months but really didn't know him at all. The gardener hadn't had a past they spoke about, he didn't have a powerful grandmother who offered threats, he didn't live in a castle and wear expensive suits. He hadn't gotten his heart broken by someone named Emilia.

Julia could picture the type of woman she likely was. Wealthy, highly educated, attractive, ambitious. Someone Mason had loved and lost. How soon had their breakup been? Was he using her as a consolation prize, finding someone the complete opposite?

"What did Gran have to tell you?" Mason asked Julia when she returned to the dining room.

She looked down at her necklace. "How much I don't deserve you."

His face changed. "She didn't say that."

"No," Julia said with a sigh, *but lately it's how I feel.* "It's like I'm getting to know you all over again."

"I'm the same man."

"Not really." She bit her lip. "Who's Emilia?"

His eyes flashed with anger. "She told you about her?"

"Not in so many words, but—"

Mason stood. "Excuse me."

She grabbed his arm. "Don't be angry. She issued a warning because she's trying to protect you."

His brows shot up. "She threatened you?"

"Mason." Julia lightly touched his cheek. "It's okay. I don't mind. I think it's sweet."

"But she made you feel like you don't belong."

"No, it's the way I feel." She looked around the room. "I'm not used to all this."

He took a deep breath. "You belong here. You belong wherever I am."

She smiled. "Sometimes you can be so romantic."

He kissed her. "Remember that."

She drew back. "But your grandmother is fierce. I see where you get that from."

"When we get back I'll formally introduce you to my mum. Fortunately, she already likes you."

He kissed her once more before he walked away and it took Julia a moment to realize he hadn't told her who Emilia was.

CHAPTER THIRTY-FOUR

"Well this is a surprise. I haven't seen you here in a while," Emilia said when she saw Mason standing on the balcony. She'd come over to Celeste's penthouse to give her some papers and been surprised that the dining area had been laid out as if she were expecting a guest.

Emilia hadn't expected it to be Mason and he wasn't wearing his usual dark trousers and brown blazer but instead looked business casual in grey wool trousers, a white shirt and navy sports coat. He didn't usually dress up to visit with his mother. Something was up.

He'd twice rejected her invitation to lunch and declined dinner. Her treat. He'd lately been distracted when they spoke on the phone; usually he hung on her every word.

He left the balcony and headed for the living room. "Been busy."

"Too busy to see Celeste? That's a rarity."

He adjusted a side table lamp. "She understands."

Emilia noticed the gesture, it also wasn't like him to straighten things, but she didn't want to question it. She rested a hand on his arm when he glanced at something behind her. He lowered his gaze to meet hers.

"What?"

Emilia lowered her voice to make sure Celeste, who had disappeared into the kitchen, couldn't overhear them. "Could I ask you a favor? Bonnie's nanny—"

"I'm afraid I can't."

She paused. She wasn't used to him interrupting her and she certainly wasn't used to him saying no. She looked over his attire once more with renewed interest.

"What's the occasion?"

Before he could reply, the doorbell rang and she watched his gaze heat up. She felt her entire body grow warm as the look of desire filled his dark eyes. It took her one blinding moment to realize that he wasn't looking at her, but at something...no someone behind her. She turned to see who had captured his interest and saw a pretty, but chubby looking black woman enter the room, dressed in a red V-neck cocktail dress and wearing a gold necklace with a strange fish pendant.

"Excuse me," Mason said before he walked past her.

Emilia caught her breath, her heart racing, wondering why she felt suddenly so bereft as if she'd lost something. He looked so different now. It had been a gradual shift but now it was stunningly clear. He was so charismatically and vitally alive. A man who could love and care with his entire being. How had she not seen it before? How had she not seen the beauty of his brown eyes? The protective stance of his body, how he always made her feel cared for? She was used to his gaze seeking hers. She'd grown accustomed to having him all to herself. But no more.

Who was this woman? Where had she come from? Celeste had been cagey about Mason's whereabouts recently. Did she know?

Emilia watched the woman smile up at Mason and he smiled down at her.

It was the smile that broke open her heart. She realized how genuine and true his smiles were. They were never a weapon used like other more handsome men. They weren't practiced and polished, they were warm and generous and they'd once been hers. She'd once been able to make him smile like that and she wanted to again. She hadn't believed she had an adversary, now that she knew she wouldn't stand still.

She realized she loved him and wanted him back. She'd made a mistake. But she wouldn't make another one.

"ARE YOU NERVOUS?" Mason asked Julia as he led her to the living room.

"No."

"Then why do you look like you've seen a ghost?"

Julia looked past him and nodded at the beautiful woman with cascading black hair, cinnamon skin and tall graceful figure, who seemed frozen in place. "Who is she?"

Celeste entered the room before he could reply. "Thank you for coming," she said with a warm smile. "I'm glad you have forgiven us our little pretense." She gestured to the elegant statue. "This is my assistant, Emilia."

Julia gasped at the name and sight of the other woman. She was more stunning than she'd imagined and she hadn't thought she'd ever have to meet her. If she'd hurt Mason so cruelly why had his stepmother hired her? How could he bear it?

"It's a pleasure to meet you," Emilia said in a cultured tone. But her brown eyes had a cold, battle-like sheen that spoke of war. Julia couldn't understand it. She could understand Mason's grandmother's warning, but not his ex. She hadn't been prepared to have a rival.

Mason rocked on his heels. "You ladies will have to try the pecan ice cream Julia once made me for dinner."

"You mean dessert," Emilia smoothly corrected.

Mason shook his head and sent Julia an affectionate grin. "No, I mean dinner. She's also great with chocolate and cookies and cream."

Julia could hardly pay attention to his praise, too aware of the other woman's venomous stare.

"Could you excuse me a minute?" Julia said, taking a quick step back. "I think I left something in my car." She turned and raced out of the apartment before anyone could stop her. She ran down the stairs, instead of taking the elevator, and hurried out the front entrance. She wouldn't go back. She couldn't go back. The women in Mason's life were scary. It was all too much.

She grabbed her keys and jumped inside her car.

She wanted a simple life.

She wished she could go back to how things had been. She started the engine then jumped when someone knocked on the driver's side window.

CHAPTER THIRTY-FIVE

Julia took a deep breath before she lowered it.

Mason stared down at her. "Where are you going?"

"I just need some fresh air."

"*Inside* your car?"

Julia turned off the engine and lowered her head. "I'm sorry."

"I don't want you to be sorry. I want you to talk to me."

Julia reluctantly rolled up the window, got out of the car and faced him. "I'm sorry."

"For what? What's wrong?"

She tugged on the skirt of her dress. "I'm overdressed, aren't I?"

Mason rested his hands on his hips and sighed. "Yes." When she looked at him alarmed he shook his head and said, "But you look beautiful. Now tell me what's wrong."

"Emilia wants you back."

Mason looked at her for a startled moment then threw his head back and laughed.

"I'm not kidding."

He grinned with delight. "You're jealous."

She frowned. "And you find that funny?"

He struggled to suppress his amusement. "No, yes, I mean..." He sighed. "Look, there's nothing to be jealous about."

Julia folded her arms. "You promised not to lie to me again."

"I'm not lying." He rested a hand over his heart. "I swear."

"Nothing to be jealous of?" Julia tapped her chin as if lost in thought. "Let's see. She's gorgeous, she's intelligent, your grandmother told me she's the one woman who broke your heart and yet she works for your stepmother. So that means you have to keep seeing her." She poked his chest with her forefinger. "Isn't that just lovely and cozy?"

Mason drummed his fingers on the hood of her car, the sound resembling the coming of thunder. "You make it sound complicated but it's not. We're family."

"Really?" She opened her car door. "Well, I'm not ready to meet any more of your family."

He closed the door with a hard bang. "She wasn't supposed to be here today."

"But it worked out for you anyway, right? You can show her that you've moved on. You can watch us vie for your affection. It must stroke your ego to have two women who want you, but I won't—"

Mason gripped her shoulders. "Julia, stop it." His

voice broke. "I know I lied but please don't hurt me like this."

"Hurt you?"

He released a long, steadying breath and stepped back from her. "Emilia has never..." His voice shook with pain. "Could never..." He turned and looked up at the sky. "She couldn't care for me like that."

"But she does."

He faced her with flashing dark eyes and a tone as hard as iron. "She doesn't."

Julia hugged herself suddenly afraid. Not afraid of his fierce denial, but of the hold Emilia still had on him. The one he didn't see. Emilia had hurt him, but he still...

She heard the sound of her keys hitting the asphalt as she realized what she didn't want to face. She'd been a diversion. He wanted to get over Emilia, but he hadn't.

Mason bent down and picked up her keys. When he held them out to her and saw the fear in her gaze, he felt rocked by a piercing anguish. He never wanted her to be afraid of him. He hadn't meant to lash out at her.

He fell to his knees, no longer wanting to loom over her. He wanted to make her feel safe with him. He wanted to make himself as small and non-threatening as he could. He hung his head and whispered, "Please don't go."

He felt her tug on his coat. "Mason, get up. Don't do this."

He kept his gaze lowered. "If I tell you everything will you promise to stay?"

"Only if you stand up first."

"It's probably better for you if I—"

She nudged him with her shoe. "No, get up."

He rose to his feet, leaned his back against her car and faced the building. "There's nothing to be jealous of." He folded his arms. "Here's a brief history. I met Emilia. I fell in love with her...I asked her to marry me...she fell in love with my stepbrother... and..." He took a deep breath. "...it hurt like a hacksaw. They got married, I accepted it. The end."

"So she's your sister-in-law?"

"Yes, no...sort of."

"What do you mean 'sort of'?"

"They got divorced but I still consider her family as does my mum. Emilia is the mother of my niece after all. The arrangement works because as a single mother we can support her and she can depend on us."

"But your family has money. What about alimony and child support? Couldn't she—"

"Emilia signed a contract before she married him. My stepbrother left her with very little."

"And you came to the rescue."

He shrugged. "It's the right thing to do."

Julia shook her head, amazed. "You're almost too good to be true."

He suddenly turned to her as a thought struck him. "Is that what this is about?"

She blinked. "What?"

His smile returned. "I know what's going on. You think everyone feels about me the way you do." His smile widened. "That's it, isn't it?"

"No, I—"

He drew her close. "That's okay. You don't have to

admit it." He kissed her then drew back and held her gaze, his brown eyes heating with longing. "But it's sexy as hell."

Julia shook her head. "Mason—"

He kissed her again before he gathered her in his arms. "I won't lie, it's a stroke to the ego. But you really don't have anything to worry about. Okay? Nod if you believe me."

Julia sighed. He didn't understand, but she didn't want to lose him. She wrapped her arms around him and nodded, although it hurt to do so.

ALL THROUGH DINNER, which included roast chicken flavored with rosemary, wine and balsamic vinegar that tasted like cardboard on Julia's numb tongue, she tried to be relaxed with his stepmother but found it difficult. She just wanted to go home and bury herself in a book and not think anymore.

"Any lingering anger or doubts you have about Mason, I hope you'll blame me," Celeste told her when they had a moment alone in the kitchen. "I was the one who pushed him. I was the one who thought of the idea for him to pretend to be the gardener. Not him. He was truly reluctant to do it."

"I understand."

She held her gaze. "I sincerely hope you do."

But Julia could still only think about escape as Mason walked her to her car.

"How about lunch tomorrow?" he said.

"I can't."

"Dinner?"

"No, I'm pretty busy this week."

"It doesn't have to be anything fancy. I'll come by and we can order—"

The sight of her car lit under the lamp of the parking lot filled Julia with relief. "I really need to focus on some projects this week. I'll call you."

"How come that sounds like you want to break up?"

She opened the car door. "I need space to think some things over, that's all."

"I'm sorry. I—"

"You've said that. You don't have to say it anymore." She kissed him on the cheek. "I will call you soon."

But she didn't.

CHAPTER THIRTY-SIX

He was going to lose her.

Mason sat back on his heels and pulled off the rubber gloves he'd used to clean Alice's large cage. He found the weekly cleaning meditative, but even more so after nearly a week not hearing from Julia.

Mason glanced at Alice who was happily perched on the back of his desk chair, whistling and talking to the rhythm of a reggae song filtering through the speakers. He'd learned she became the chattiest when he played either reggae or country.

He turned his attention back to the new clean cage and reattached the colorful ladder and replaced the tiny balls that Alice enjoyed playing with before he added water to the bird bath. He knew he could mist her to keep her clean, but Alice liked to go under the water for fun. He hoped one day Julia would take a picture of that.

If he hadn't already lost her.

Mason shook his head. No, he wouldn't think that

way. She needed space, that's what she'd told him. He had to believe her. But she was wavering. That was the danger. If he didn't do something soon someone else could take her away.

He pulled out his cell phone. "Think I should send her flowers?" he asked the little bird.

Alice whistled then replied, "Backside!"

"Yes, you're right. That's too cliché."

He tapped his shoulder and the budgie flew and landed on it. "How about another necklace?"

Alice chirped again. "Mawga dog. Mawga dog."

"Right, I've already given her jewelry and travel. Don't want to repeat too soon." He moved his shoulders up and down in a motion that Alice liked. She bobbed her head up and down in sequence. "What else could she want?"

Alice flapped her wings and chatted words in such a quick succession they sounded garbled.

Mason nodded, still moving his shoulders in rhythm to the music. "Yes. Her car's old. Maybe needs work. That's something." He pulled out his cell phone and scrolled for different options.

"What are you doing?" Tracy asked.

Mason spun around startled. "Don't you know how to knock?"

She closed the door and mimicked the way he'd been moving his shoulders. "I did knock. You were too busy dancing to hear."

He felt heat crawl up his neck. He set his cell phone down on the desk. "What do you want?"

"What are you doing?"

He placed Alice back in her cage. "None of your business."

She looked at the images on his cell phone. "These models are too small for you." She paused. "But it isn't for you, is it?"

Mason tucked his cell phone away and looked at her bored. "Did you come here for something?"

"You're thinking of buying her a car? Did she ask for it?"

"No."

"Then why?"

He shrugged.

Tracy threw up her hands, exasperated. "You're doing it again. Anytime something goes wrong you think of throwing money at the problem. What happened?"

"Aside from the fact that she found out I've been lying to her?"

Tracy sighed. "She seemed fine in England and Aunty told me dinner went well. You told us she'd forgiven you."

He sat in his favorite chair and sighed, glancing at the empty space where the book *Return to Love* had been. She had yet to give it back to him. "I think she got the wrong idea about Emilia."

Tracy sat down intrigue. "What kind of idea?"

"That she—" Mason paused. He didn't want to share Julia's thoughts about Emilia having feelings for him. As absurd as it was he didn't want his cousin laughing at him. "It's stupid.

"But if it's bothering her then it's important."

"I'll figure something out."

"Buying her a car won't fix things."

"It's better than doing nothing." He pulled out his cell phone. "I have to get her to trust me."

"What if that's not the problem?"

Mason looked at her resigned. "You mean the problem is me?"

Tracy jumped up, grabbed his shoulders and shook him. Or at least tried to. He barely moved.

Mason leaned back in his chair and looked up at her confused. "What are you doing?"

"Trying to shake some sense into you." She adjusted her glasses. "But that's impossible since you weigh a ton."

He gently shoved her away and glanced around the room. "I need to spray this room for mosquitoes." His gaze settled on her face. "They're awful pests."

She stuck out her tongue. "I didn't say the problem was you, but it might be something else."

"I don't care what it is as long as I can persuade her to stay by my side. I don't want to lose her. I have to fix this."

"Give her time. Maybe there's nothing to fix. It is a lot to take in." Tracy hesitated then said, "Especially Emilia."

Mason rubbed his chin and said in a low voice, "I wish I knew what Gran said to her."

Tracy cleared her throat. "Did Julia say anything about Emilia?"

Something too stupid to share. "Not really."

"Oh."

He looked at her, his gaze sharpened. "You sound surprised. Why?"

"No reason."

"Why would she?"

"She's part of your past. You...loved her."

"And she left me."

Tracy opened her mouth then closed it.

"What? If you have something to say, then say it."

"Never mind. It's nothing." Tracy pointed at him. "Just don't buy her a car."

CHAPTER THIRTY-SEVEN

Chloe stared at Julia open-mouthed. They sat in Julia's apartment with a bucket of spicy Buffalo wings, fries and soda. The items crowded the surface of the coffee table.

She had only meant to tell her friend about Mason's true identity, but found herself also discussing her trip to Kenya then England and meeting his grandmother and how his ex-girlfriend worked for his mother.

Chloe licked her fingers. "Wait, you were seeing someone and didn't tell me?"

"I was going to."

"And when I texted you about getting together for lunch and you said you were busy you were actually in Kenya?"

"It was an unexpected trip."

"That he paid for."

Julia nodded. "Yes."

Chloe picked up a buffalo wing, took a bite then

pointed it at her. "Don't even think about it," she mumbled.

"What?"

"You are not allowed to break up with him."

Julia took a sip of her soda annoyed her friend had guessed what she had been thinking. "Why not?"

"Because he sounds amazing and perfect for you."

Julia shook her head. "Maybe, but if you saw Emilia—"

Chloe finished the buffalo wing and licked her fingers again. "But he's dating *you*. He says she's part of his past."

"If you saw the way she looked at him." Julia patted her chest. "The way she looked at me."

Chloe held out both hands, her fingers covered in red sauce. "I don't care." She grabbed a napkin and wiped her fingers. "You're coming up with excuses to hide again."

"I don't hide."

"Then why are you trying to push him away?"

"I'm not. I just need time to think."

"There's nothing to think about. He's got a family and an ex. So what? It's not a crime. You didn't expect his life to be perfect, right?" Chloe tossed the napkin on the table next to two other discarded ones. "Does he know about your ex?"

"No need. He'll never meet him."

"Does he know about—?"

"Again no need." Julia sighed. "Before all this it was simple between us. Nice."

"It wasn't real."

Julia frowned. "I know that now."

"But that doesn't mean *he* isn't." Chloe sighed then made a wide sweeping gesture of the room. "Before you met him you didn't have one living thing in your house. Not a plant or a pet. Nothing. Now you have these beautiful plants, even you couldn't kill, that brighten up your place. How many books have you read this week?"

"I don't know. Maybe two."

Chloe snapped her fingers. "Exactly. You're living again too, instead of hiding in a book. He's good for you. Don't ruin it."

Julia thought of her friend's words a half hour later as she sat alone in her apartment, the scent of hot sauce still scenting the air, and stared at the spider plant near the couch. She took out her cell phone and looked at the picture she'd taken of Mason with his back to her, staring at a flock of flamingoes.

She'd tried to get a picture of him, but when she'd told him to look at her he'd turn around, holding his hand over his face. She remembered being irritated with him for ruining her shot and the delighted sound of his laughter.

Staring at the photo brought back the memory with clarity. It was a perfectly captured moments she could revisit over and over again. That was why she preferred photographs and books, why they had been her sanctuary. They were safe and never changing. She could always revisit them and know what they were about, and relive the feelings they ignited. But people weren't like that.

Marriages fell apart. Careers ended. Hopes and dreams died. She'd had enough chaos with her father, she didn't want it again. She wanted order. She wanted something she could understand.

Mark had been easy to understand. He had simple pleasures and a simple life.

But Mark was gone. Mason had taken his place.

Mason was a man who lived in a castle. A man who had a gorgeous ex-girlfriend and lots of money. Mason was a man who felt out of reach.

Chloe was right. She was afraid and wanted to hide. He felt as elusive as her dream to be a photographer. She didn't want to reach for something and fail again. The pain would hurt even more.

You mean more to me than you know.

She wanted to believe his words. She missed him. Whatever he called himself she missed being with him. That hadn't changed. She felt comfortable with him. She liked when he smiled and how he could make her laugh.

Julia felt the sting of tears and their slow descent down her face. She'd already lost something important. She'd lost her heart. She couldn't protect herself. He'd snuck in without her knowing. She couldn't walk away as much as she wanted to.

She couldn't capture him in a moment, trap him in time. A photograph of him wouldn't be enough to sustain her.

She looked at the ruined photo again. Mason had

managed to cover his face, but not his smile. His bright white teeth shone through.

She loved his smile.

She wanted him. She wanted to experience life with him. She wanted to inhale the lingering scent of raspberry that seemed to cling to him, feel the touch of his hand, taste mint chocolate chip ice cream on his lips. He may still love Emilia, but she didn't want to be stuck again. He had brought life into her life and she wanted to live it.

Julia stood ready to call him, but then stopped when her father called her instead.

CHAPTER THIRTY-EIGHT

He didn't care if she got angry. He was ready for it. A week was long. Nearly two was agonizing. He wouldn't let her avoid him. Mason rang Julia's doorbell and stood back ready for her wrath. Instead the door slowly creaked open and a puffy eye peeked out through the crack in the door.

"Hello?" Julia said in a hoarse voice.

His annoyance turned to worry. "Are you all right?"

"Yeah."

"Let me in."

"You shouldn't. I—"

"I can push my way in if you want."

"Or blow my house down like the big bad wolf?"

"What?"

"Never mind." Julia sighed and opened the door wider.

Mason stared, shocked by the sight of her. She looked

awful. Puffy eyes, dull skin. He touched her forehead. "You're burning up. You should have called me."

"It's nothing. My dad had a cold and was kind enough to share it with me when he asked me to run some errands for him."

"Lie down."

"I don't want you to catch it."

"I said lie down."

Julia sat on the couch and pulled covers over herself. In the corner he saw she'd been working on an image of a deflated balloon in a field, and she'd added colorful swirls to give it a surreal feeling.

Seeing the photo reminded him of someone or something. He wasn't quite sure which or why. But her picture gave him a vague, hazy feeling of something familiar. Her work usually did and he couldn't understand why.

He brushed the sensation aside. He didn't need to analyze right now. All he knew was that he liked her creative visions and couldn't understand why she wouldn't let him frame any of them and put them on the wall.

He walked to the kitchen and opened the fridge. It was empty. "When was the last time you ate or drank something?"

"I don't know. I had to do some accounting for my Dad..."

Mason slammed the door closed. Not only did he need to restock her fridge he needed to address a major problem. "I'll be right back."

~

NOLAN LESTER REMEMBERED EXACTLY where he was that relatively calm day September 11, 2001 when the world changed for him and millions of others.

When a large, fierce looking black man, with eyes as cool as the autumn breeze arrived at his office door, the same feeling of dread seized him.

Life, as he knew it, would never be the same.

Mason saw fear in the older man's eyes and did nothing to dispel it. He wanted Nolan to be afraid. Very afraid.

He pushed his way into the office without invitation and swept a glance around the cramped room, letting his gaze briefly linger on the photos on the wall: happy couples, a dramatic showdown between police and a crowd, the devastation of loss left by a natural disaster. He folded his arms. "This your work?"

Nolan nodded, stroking his white beard with pride. "Yes. I'm a photographer."

Mason shifted his gaze from the walls to the two desks that faced each other. One had a metal fold up chair while the other boasted a plush cloth covered swivel chair. "Just you?" he asked, careful to keep his voice neutral, though he could feel his anger rising. He knew exactly which desk belonged to Julia.

"Yes." Nolan followed Mason's look and said, "My daughter helps me but she's not a professional." He gestured to one of the two client chairs. "Would you like to take a seat?"

Mason nodded and sat behind Nolan's desk. He faced the man daring him to challenge his choice.

Nolan meekly sunk into one of the chairs facing the desk. "Is this about the money? Did they send you?" he asked in a trembling voice. "Listen I can pay. My daughter has a boyfriend and from what my other daughter tells me he's loaded. I've asked her to tap him, but she won't. But if she knew you were here, I'm sure that would change her mind."

Mason leaned back in the chair in an effort to ease his anger, the chair groaned under his weight. *This* was the man indebted to his mother? Julia was pawning jewelry, taking extra jobs and selling what she could find to pay off the debt for *this* man? One who was making no attempt to take responsibility even after he'd been given a reprieve?

Mason flexed his hands to keep from gripping them into a fist. He nodded. "That sounds like a good idea."

Nolan sighed relieved.

"There's just one problem."

He blinked. "What?"

Mason leaned forward, clasping his hands together on the desk. His voice turned to ice. "I'm the boyfriend."

Nolan's eyes widened in renewed fear.

"That puts you in a very bad spot. You're disrespecting two people I care about."

Nolan licked his lips. He pressed his hands together, pleading for understanding. "I wouldn't...I've tried but I have bills and a divorce and—"

Mason waved his hand. "I don't care."

"But—"

Mason stood and came from behind the desk. "This

is what you're going to do. You're going to start spoiling your daughter. Every time Julia tells me about something nice you've done for her, I'll take a thousand off what you owe."

Nolan stared at him outraged. "Nice? I've always done something nice for Julia."

Mason marched past him and picked up the metal chair. He folded it up and threw it on the ground, where it clattered like a loud echoing boom. "You call that nice? Right now she's home sick with hardly any food in her fridge. Did you once think to check on her?"

Nolan shrugged. "It's a little cold. She'll be fine."

He pointed to the desk. "You have two pictures on your desk and not one of those women is Julia."

"I see her almost every day, why would I need a picture?" Nolan lifted a picture of Myla. "She likes having her picture taken, Julia doesn't." He lifted the picture of Evelyn. "And my wife's—uh, ex-wife's smug face motivates me to do better."

"How about the walls?"

"The walls?"

"How come you don't even have one of Julia's pictures on the wall? Even a small four by seven?"

"Because it's *my* office. *My* business. I'm the professional not her."

The venom in the older man's voice didn't surprise him. There was something sinister hidden behind the kindly white beard and brown eyes. Something few people could see. Especially Julia. "Do you still want to *have* a business?" Mason said in a soft tone.

Nolan sagged defeated. "What do you want?"

Mason walked to the door. "You heard me the first time. I won't repeat myself." He opened the door. "I'd better hear Julia singing your praises soon or I'll make sure my mother adds interest."

CHAPTER THIRTY-NINE

It was such a pleasant dream.

Julia dreamt Mason came by and gave her a bowl of the most delicious chicken noodle soup she'd ever had and then he tucked her into bed. He checked her temperature and lectured her on not calling him, but he was being so sweet she didn't care. She was just glad that he was there. That she wasn't alone. "I missed you so much."

"You should have called me," he said.

"I was afraid."

"Why?"

"Because I don't want to bother you."

"Better to bother me than annoy me. I hate being annoyed."

Funny she'd never imagine him saying that, her mind really was creative. "I'm sorry."

"Good."

"Are you mad at me?"

"Two weeks. You didn't call for nearly two weeks! Not a text. A message. Email. Sky writing. Nothing."

He really sounded upset. She couldn't remember him ever being like that. She would have thought in her dream he'd be more understanding. Julia sighed. It didn't matter. He was there and she could indulge in her fantasy a little while longer before he faded into her memory. Strange how she could dream about drifting off to sleep.

THE NEXT MORNING she woke up feeling much better. She was shocked to see how clean her bedroom was and it felt fresher. She grabbed a robe and walked into the hall. She was hungry and the aroma of roasted bell peppers and cheese didn't help. Someone from another apartment must be cooking something nice.

She walked into the kitchen and screamed.

Mason sighed. He rested against the kitchen counter with his arms folded. "I really wish you wouldn't do that."

She gathered her robe tighter. "What are you doing here?"

"I've been here."

"No you haven't. I mean I dreamt that..." Julia covered her mouth as her eyes widened. "You were really here?"

He nodded. "You become really chatty when you're sick."

"It was nothing."

"So you didn't miss me?"

She hesitated.

He pushed himself from the counter. "Never mind. You don't have to answer that. Hungry?"

She nodded before she looked him up and down. "Enough that I probably could eat you."

A quick grin softened his face. "Maybe later." He motioned to the table.

She sat and continued to stare at him as he placed an omelet in front of her.

"Did you make this?"

"I poured you a glass of orange juice. That's about the extent of my culinary skills." He lowered his voice and winked. "I've got connections."

Julia took a bite and moaned in pleasure. "It's delicious."

He sat down.

"You're not going to eat?"

"I already did."

He placed his hand palm up on the table.

Julia took another large bite and shook her head. "I'm not touching you until I'm not infectious."

"Too late. You were all over me last night."

"No, I wasn't."

"You gripped my hand. I couldn't leave if I wanted to."

"Sorry about that."

"Don't be sorry." He lifted an eyebrow and deepened his voice. "I liked it."

Julia lowered her gaze, desperate to focus on her food. If he continued to look at her like that she might be all over him again.

Mason leaned back in his seat. "I have an event coming up and I want you there. Tracy's hosting a fundraiser for a non-profit she works with."

"No problem." Julia took a long swallow of her orange juice glad she felt human again. "What's the set up? What do you want me to focus on?"

Mason frowned. "I don't want you as a photographer. I want you as my date."

"Oh, but—"

"If you're worried about what to wear, tell me what you want and I'll buy it for you."

"Thanks, but—"

"Hair and makeup too."

"Mason, I—"

"No excuses. I want to show my girlfriend off."

"Mason—"

"I understand if you want to take things slow."

Julia set her utensils down on the table with a bang. "Will you be quiet and let me speak?"

He nodded.

"I'm sorry I didn't contact you. I'm glad you're here and," she picked up her fork, "you might regret offering to buy me a dress."

A slow smile spread on his lips. "I have a feeling it will be worth it."

CHAPTER FORTY

Emilia didn't like when a man was distracted in her presence. Especially if that man was Mason. He'd dropped by to update Celeste on a proposed minor renovation at the castle. But once Celeste excused herself to take a phone call in the other room, Emilia found Mason standing in the living room smiling at something on his cell phone. He'd usually take the opportunity to ask her how she was doing.

She walked up to him. "What are you looking at?"

"Julia's sending me pictures of the dresses she's trying on."

Emilia stepped closer, but the way he stood made it difficult for her to see. "What do you think?"

"I think she should buy all three."

Emilia felt a wave of envy. She rested a hand on his arm before he could text back a reply. "That's not helpful, which one would you really like?"

He shrugged. "Whatever she likes."

"You're talking to me. Be honest."

Mason looked through the selection again and said, "The green one."

Celeste's voice interrupted her response. "Mason, could you show me those numbers again?"

He set the phone down and picked up his notepad before he left the room.

Emilia took the opportunity to pick up his cell phone to see what Julia had sent him. She looked at the selection and sniffed. She could wear each dress better.

Which do you like? Julia texted.

Get all three. Emilia began to type, remembering Mason's words. Then she paused and erased that message as a new thought struck her. She bit her lip, her pulse quickening and typed, *Get the green one.*

Okay.

Emilia grinned and deleted the exchange before she set the cell phone down.

CHAPTER FORTY-ONE

Of course she'd be wearing the same dress.

Julia stood in the entrance of the ballroom and spotted Mason talking with Emilia and Tracy at the front of the room under the large banner displaying the organization's name. Both Mason and Emilia were hard to miss. Mason because he was the largest man in the room and Emilia because she was arguably the most beautiful.

Julia had had to help her father with some book-keeping so she hadn't been able to arrive at the event with Mason. She realized that had been a mistake.

Emilia wore a green dress that matched hers exactly, except Emilia looked like she'd stepped off a runway.

Julia swallowed and took a deep breath. Don't run. Don't hide. He asked you here. You belong.

She began to make her way towards him then stopped when he turned and saw her. The expression on his face wiped away any feeling of being self-conscious and made her entire body grow warm. He said something to the two women before he made his way to her.

His heated gaze swept over her dress. "You look stunning. You picked my favorite. Are you a mind reader?"

She frowned. "You're the one who told me you liked it."

"I did?" He shook his head. "I don't remember. Turn around for me."

Julia slowly did then laughed, feeling silly that she'd worried at all. "Well lucky you. You have two women wearing your favorite dress."

Mason furrowed his brows. "Two?"

She stole a glance at the woman who was watching him. "Emilia is wearing the same dress."

Mason turned with disinterest. "She is?"

Julia blinked. "You can't tell?"

"I know you're both wearing green, but that's it." His voice deepened. "Doesn't matter. I like yours better."

Julia laughed. Point one for her. "Oh, and my father told me he's figured out a way to pay back the loan."

"Hmm."

"I don't know what's gotten into him, but he's really changed. He seems more mature somehow. He got me a new chair for the office and even bought me this bracelet." She held out her wrist for Mason to see.

He nodded in approval. "Nice."

She studied the bracelet, baffled. "I think so too. For some reason he was very insistent that I show you."

Mason took her hand. "Let's not talk about your father right now. Let's dance."

Everything fell away when he pulled her into a

dancer's embrace. Their eyes met and she let the sensual rhythm of the music sweep through her, reveling in the warm heat of his body close to hers. She mouthed the words to the love ballad the DJ played, her heart lifting when his mouth softened into a smile.

She felt like she did when she'd first started photography and the world held promise. She had sought this feeling of belonging and now she had it.

Mason didn't make her feel odd. She knew they likely made an odd pair on the dance floor but he moved well and she matched him and it felt liberating to be in his arms and not care what people thought. She didn't care about Emilia.

She knew that she wouldn't let him go, she'd fight for him. She'd fight for this.

TRACY COULDN'T STOP a smile as she watched the couple, lost in each other's gaze, on the dance floor. "Round one. Julia."

Emilia glared at her. "Shut up."

"Why are you even here? You rarely come to these events."

Emilia grabbed a glass of wine from a passing waitress. She took a sip. "Celeste couldn't make it and asked me to come instead."

"Pity."

She shot her a glance before she took another long sip. "You never liked me."

Tracy clicked her tongue. "I only wish Mason had felt the same."

"I loved him. I just—"

"Loved Gavin's looks and money more."

Emilia shook her head. "No, that's not true. He fooled me."

Tracy adjusted her glasses and scowled. "And too late you've realized what you've lost and want it back again."

Emilia gripped the wine glass. "It's not too late."

Tracy returned her gaze to the couple on the dance floor. "I'd say it is."

CHAPTER FORTY-TWO

Absolute bliss. Julia rested her head on Mason's bare chest and let her gaze sweep over the large chandelier, gilded side table and white and gold tufted chaise lounge in Mason's bedroom. Many of the ornamental pillows that had been on his bed now lay scattered on the carpet near her green dress. She moved her shoulders and felt the soft satin of his blankets shift against her skin.

Never in a million years would she have dreamt she would have made love in a room like this. With a man like this.

"How come you don't show your work?" Mason asked her as he lazily stroked her back.

She stiffened and closed her eyes. Why did he have to ruin a perfect moment?

"Julia?"

She squeezed her eyes tighter. She didn't want to talk

about it, but knew she had to. She knew about his life, it was time she shared more of hers.

She cleared her throat. "I did once. Long ago." She paused. "It was a disaster."

Mason didn't move. He could sense this was important to her and he didn't want to say anything to stop her from sharing. After a few seconds passed he wondered if that was all she would tell him when she sighed and said, "I had this teacher. I considered him a mentor really. He was, probably still is, dynamic. Talented. Amazing. I felt so lucky to be in his class and he took me under his wing, you know. Even though my father also liked photography our tastes were so different it wasn't something we could really bond on and he wasn't the most patient of teachers so…

"It was a class I took on the side while I helped my Dad. I won't lie. I had grandiose ideas. I was going to be this amazing street photographer. That's my passion. Most street photographers focus on people, but I like— liked—to focus on what people leave behind. What signs of humanity looks like. I used to save my money so that I could travel to different cities and get different perspectives. I had a lot of fun back then. When I didn't know any better."

She paused. "He said I had potential. Offered to show my work. I even had a gallery showing, if you can believe it. More than one. With the first one I could only stay about ten minutes I felt too exposed seeing other people looking at my work. My sister and mother were very supportive, my father didn't quite understand it but I think he was proud of me as well. But I couldn't stay and I didn't attend the other gallery showings either and I'm glad I didn't because in total I sold a whopping three images. One bought by my sister and the other by a friend. That was it."

"I'm sure there weren't enough people—"

"There were enough people just not enough interest. The work wasn't good."

"You don't know that."

"Yes, I do. A critic said that my work was quote a valiant attempt at a bold vision that failed to hit its mark unquote."

"Critics don't know anything."

Julia laughed but the sound was sad. "That's how I felt at first too. I told my teacher so and he said that, and I'm paraphrasing this, I had potential but no real talent. That I had what amounted to a juvenile attempt at composition, no subtly and that I was just a girl with a camera who wanted to pretend she was something special."

"And you believed him?"

"Not completely. I wasn't 'a girl' I was a fully grown woman."

Mason shook his head. "Julia, I mean it."

"Three gallery showings don't lie."

"But—"

"I answered your question and that's all I want to say about it."

Mason fell quiet a moment then said, "I like your work. Sell one to me."

"I'm not selling a picture to you."

"Why not?"

"Just tell me which one you want and I'll give it to you."

"But I want to buy it."

"No. I've already taken money from you. This would be a gift."

He sighed. "Fine. I like the image of the lost shoe among scattered autumn leaves."

He felt her smile. "I really like that one too. I'll get it framed for you."

"Hmm." It was the only thing he was able to manage. He was angry. Something didn't feel right. Julia's work was good, there was no way she'd only sold three at three gallery showings.

"Who managed the galleries? The sales? Did you get receipts? How were things itemized? How were your shows marketed?"

"I don't know. My teacher took care of that. He had people in the industry. Once, he actually paid people to show up. It was that bad."

"You let him handle everything? You didn't question whether—"

"No." She lightly tapped him on the chest. "Please don't be mad at me."

He took a deep breath. "I'm not mad."

"You sound angry. You get this low growl in your voice when you are."

His voice deepened. "I'm not," he said, but he was lying and she knew it. But he wasn't mad at her. "I'm just thinking about something." *Like how I can wheedle the name of your damn teacher and make him explain a few things.*

"Okay, fine. If it makes you feel better I'll charge you a dollar."

"Don't insult your work."

Julia placed a kiss on his chest. "Let's not talk about it anymore."

Mason drew her closer and nodded. He wouldn't talk, he would act.

CHAPTER FORTY-THREE

Julia glanced at her watch and finished her second breadstick. She looked around the bustling Italian restaurant wondering how much longer she'd have to wait for Mason to arrive. She felt a burst of autumn wind when a well dressed couple came through the front entrance. She notice a yellow leaf attached to the boot of the man's shoe.

She became so entranced by the image, wondering how she would frame it if she had her camera with her, that she didn't notice Mason had arrived until she heard him place something on the table. She turned and saw a cheque made out to her. She looked at it confused. "What's this?"

Mason sat down, sounding pleased. "It's yours. I know I could have sent the money to your account, but I thought this was better."

She looked up at him. "But what is it for?"

"I sold your picture. I hope you don't mind, but a friend of mine really liked it so I couldn't say no."

She'd given him the picture only a week ago. Julia lifted up the cheque and stared at the amount. "You shouldn't have done this. I don't need you to bully your friends to buy my work."

"I didn't bully anyone."

"You're really going to tell me that someone bought my photo for two thousand dollars?"

He shrugged. "I know it isn't much, but—"

Her brows shot up. "Isn't much? Maybe not to people like you, but that's a lot for a little photograph."

"I don't understand."

"I don't need pity purchases."

"Pity purchases?"

"What I told you the other night wasn't for sympathy." She waved the cheque. "Did you threaten them?"

He looked hurt. "I didn't bully or threaten anyone. She liked it as much as I did. What kind of man do you think I am? I thought you knew me better than that."

She felt embarrassed. He was right. That wasn't like him. "I'm sorry. It's just. My work is average. I accept that. I don't need you to pretend and make me feel better."

"I'm not pretending. I hired you the first time because I liked your work."

"I know but—"

"I think it's better than you think. Why will you believe your teacher over me?"

She forced a smile. "I think you're a little biased."

He didn't smile back. "No, I'm not." He leaned forward. "What's his name? Can I see his work?"

"No, he doesn't have a website."

His jaw twitched. His eyes darkened. "You're lying."

"I know."

"Why won't you tell me his name?"

"Because right now you look like a man who's ready to order a hit. One that's fast, clean and won't leave a trace."

Mason leaned back and narrowed his eyes, but didn't say anything.

Julia held out the cheque.

His voice hardened. "Keep it. I don't care what you do with it." He stood.

She stared up at him, surprised. "Where are you going?"

"I'm going to pay."

She looked at the nearly empty bread basket. "We haven't even ordered anything."

"I'm not hungry. Order what you want and take your time. I'll meet you out front." He left.

Furious. He was furious with her and that was the last thing she'd wanted. She looked at the menu and swore. She'd lost her appetite too. She caught the eye of a waiter. "You can clear the table for someone else," she said before she left and went into the ladies' room.

She looked down at the cheque and felt tears swell. If only it had been real. But she had no right to get mad at him. He was only trying to help.

Garbage. That was what her teacher had called one of her projects.

She'd never tell Mason that.

"Are you okay?" a soft voice asked.

Julia wiped her tears away embarrassed. "Yes, I'm fine. Sorry."

"Are you sure you're okay? Do you want me to call anyone?"

She frowned. "Call?"

"I saw you with that...man. Did he threaten you? You looked very upset."

"Oh no," Julia said quickly. "It was nothing like that."

The woman looked doubtful.

"Truly."

She lightly patted Julia on the back. "As long as you're okay."

"I'm fine. Thanks." Julia hurried out of the ladies' room feeling even more miserable than before. Mason was the most generous, kindhearted man she'd ever known and people saw him otherwise. She walked out of the restaurant and saw him standing by a large oak tree, its orange and yellow leaves shaded part of the building in a canopy of color.

She watched as others cast suspicious wary looks in his direction, others gave him a wide berth. There were few who passed by without noticing the large man standing in quiet misery.

She wanted to shout and defend him. He may look fierce, and as he stood there with his arms folded, dressed in black, he looked especially so, but he was nothing like his looks, he was so much more than that. She was sorry she'd angered him. More so that she'd hurt him. She hadn't meant to do so.

She walked up to him. "Sorry I took so long."

He turned to her and frowned. "Is that supposed to be a joke?"

She saw the woman from the bathroom send her a worried look. Julia took Mason's hand then motioned him to bend towards her so she could place a kiss on his cheek. She saw the woman frown. She probably thought the show of affection was forced, but Julia didn't care. She wanted to show her that she chose to be with him. That he wasn't what he seemed.

"What was that for?" he asked her.

"An apology. I shouldn't have said those things to you."

He flashed a shy grin and squeezed her hand in affection. "Apology accepted. So if I were able to sell other photographs—"

"Don't get ahead of yourself."

He laughed then said, "I'm going to continue to do this until I get you to believe me."

"You'll have to try very hard."

"Don't worry, I intend to."

CHAPTER FORTY-FOUR

The anger still burned.

Mason parked in front of his cousin's townhouse still angered that Julia didn't realize the value of her work. He was going to get a name out of her if it was the last thing he did.

He walked up the front steps and pounded on the door.

Tracy opened it and stared at him stunned. "What's gotten into you?"

"What do you mean? You called me over to look over some contracts and—"

"Are you trying to knock my house down?"

He rested his hands on his hips in no mood for games. "No."

"Then what's this?" She pointed to the dent in the door. The one he'd made with his fist.

He rubbed the back of his neck, chagrined. He hadn't

meant to take his anger out on it. "Sorry. I'll get you a new one."

She turned. "I'd rather you tell me what's wrong."

"It's nothing," he said. Nothing except the fact that Julia believed some teacher over him and thought he'd used his position to bully people to get his way.

Mason closed the door behind him, but with enough force that the umbrella stand close by toppled to the ground.

"Don't touch it," Tracy warned him when he bent to straighten it. "Just go into the living room and don't touch anything."

He cleared his throat. "Sorry."

He went to his cousin's living room and paused. There it was. He'd seen this surrealistic photograph numerous times and never made the connection. It was one item his cousin had splurged on. He pointed. "Who did this?"

Tracy grinned. "You're into photos now?"

"Who?"

"You're not getting it."

"I know that picture."

Tracy clapped her hands as if he'd achieved an amazing feat. "Of course you do." She let her hands fall. "You've seen it a couple thousand times and you're now just realizing it?"

"I think I know the photographer."

"That's impossible."

He turned to her. "Why is it impossible?"

"Because the photographer is dead. Very tragic. She

did her work under the name Della. One day she stepped in front of train in Bangladesh—"

"Why Bangladesh?"

"Who knows? Anyway, that was it. There are only a few of her work left. You wouldn't believe what I paid for this."

"Where did you get it?"

"A friend of a friend."

"I want to know who this friend is."

"Why?" Tracy frowned. "Don't cause trouble for me."

"Why would you think I'd cause trouble?"

"Because you have that look on your face."

"I always have this look on my face."

Tracy shook her head, grave. "Not like this. Sit down and tell me what's going on."

Mason sighed and did. "I think that picture is one of Julia's work and someone ripped her off."

"Julia? No way. She does nice commercial work and I saw some of her work online, but it's not like this. This has a different artistic majesty."

"I've seen others like this. On her computer. This is what she used to do." He walked up to the photograph. "I'm sure this is hers."

"If what you're thinking is real, she's lost thousands of dollars maybe more. A friend of mine bought the license for using this image on an album cover and in stage design. There are pillows, beddings and prints based on this too."

He swore.

"What are you going to do?"

He pulled out his cell phone and took a picture. "First, find out if my hunch is right."

"And then?"

He flashed a ruthless smile. "Make someone regret they ever met me."

CHAPTER FORTY-FIVE

P art of him hoped he was wrong.

Mason sat in Julia's apartment and watched her face as she looked at the image on his cell phone, while they sat on the couch together.

Part of him wanted her to look at the photograph and deny it was hers. However, another part of him wanted to be vindicated, wanted the chance to prove that he was right about her work. But he didn't want it at this price. He didn't want to see her hurt. But when he saw the look of recognition on her face his heart swelled before it sunk because he knew what had to come next.

"Where did you see this?" Julia asked him. "This must have been the one other photograph I eventually sold."

He bit his lip. "You've sold more than one photograph."

She rolled her eyes. "My mother and sister don't count."

"I know. I'm not counting them either."

"I don't know what you mean."

"Your teacher has been selling your work over the past several years."

"No, you've got it all wrong."

"I'm not wrong. This photo was on Tracy's wall and has been there for three years. You told me you stopped five years ago."

"But—"

"There's proof that he's licensed your work without your knowledge. My question is what do you want me to do about it?"

"Do?"

"I can help, but this has to be your fight. Will you give me permission to go after him?"

"I don't know how..." She chewed her lip. "I don't see..." She sighed. "I don't understand. My work isn't even that good."

Mason pounded the coffee table, startling her. "He wanted you to believe that so that he could exploit you. Did you give him photos like you offered to give me?"

She shrugged. "Sure, a few as a thanks. He was kind enough—"

Mason rubbed his eyes and groaned. "He wasn't being kind. He was using you."

Julia set the cell phone down. Mason kept talking but she couldn't hear his words because she felt like a fool. All this time her teacher had been using her, selling her work, telling her she was worthless and she'd believed him. She'd taken pride in being independent, making her own way and she'd been duped. She was as silly and gullible as her father.

"It's not your fault," she heard Mason say.

"But I feel so stupid. I guess it's his right to sell them. I gave him permission."

"For everything?"

"No, not everything, but some—"

"We're going after him. He made up a story that you're dead so that he could up the price of your work. This is fraud. You have a right to compensation. If nothing else, you need to set the record straight. You have a reputation you can use to sell more work. But you have to be willing to fight."

She wasn't sure. She'd been closed off for so long. She'd buried the dream so many years ago, she was afraid to hope again. That's what Mason continued to give her—hope, and it was intoxicating. She felt a little spark again.

She wasn't alone. She had someone on her side to help her fight. "I'm willing. I'm ready to see him pay."

But although she was ready to fight, Julia couldn't sleep that night. Her mind was too wound up to give her rest. Her work had been selling? People had liked her photographs? Mason would fight to find out the truth for her?

She turned her head on the pillow and looked at him, sleeping beside her.

She couldn't believe how much he'd believed in her

when she'd stopped believing in herself. How much he'd given her. How much she never wanted him to leave her side.

She ran her finger down the slope of his nose. "Marry me," she whispered.

"Okay," he replied in a sleepy voice.

She paused, partly shocked that she'd asked him and partly shocked that he'd replied. He was half-asleep. He must not have heard her correctly. He probably thought she'd asked him something else. She wouldn't repeat it. She wouldn't want to embarrass herself. It wasn't like her to be so reckless. She kissed the tips of her fingers then pressed them against his cheek. Being his wife was a nice thought anyway, even though she knew it couldn't be true.

The next morning at breakfast she watched him as they both finished a bowl of granola cereal.

He didn't seem to remember last night. That was a relief. Just as she'd suspected, he'd been half asleep.

"Why do you keep staring at me like that?"

She lowered her gaze. "No reason."

He grinned and winked. "Do I suddenly look different now that I'm your fiancé?"

Her head shot up. "What? You heard me last night?"

"Of course I heard you. Why do you think I replied?"

"I thought you were dreaming."

"Me too." He hesitated. "Wait, have you changed your mind already?" He set his spoon down, his gaze uncertain. "That isn't fair."

"No, I—" She wagged her finger at him. "This is why your mother is worried about you."

"Worried about me?"

"Yes, because you're too good. Do you know how important marriage is to someone like you?"

"Someone like me?"

"Yes, of course there will have to be a prenup."

"There will be no prenup."

"We will have one otherwise I won't marry you. I won't have people whispering that I only married you for your money."

"So what? I don't care if you do."

"You're not taking this seriously."

"As long as you're willing to marry me you can take your paranoia as far as it will take you."

"I'm not being paranoid." She looked around her. "My apartment could fit inside your bedroom. No, your bathroom."

"So what?"

"You're wealthy and successful."

"Exactly, I know business." He flashed a wolfish grin. "And I know how to protect my assets. I'm not naïve."

She believed him, but his decision still felt impulsive. "What do I have to offer in exchange?"

"I'll get to be the husband of an internationally recognized photographer."

"That hasn't happened."

"Give me time and it will." He hesitated, his dark gaze suddenly uncertain. "I'd also have a wonderful woman as the mother of my children."

"You want kids?"

He nodded. "Don't you?"

Julia paused. She wasn't sure she'd ever seen him so

tense before. Fatherhood. This was a subject that meant a lot to him. She supposed it would, considering how close he'd been to his own father. She knew he would make a wonderful parent. She rested her chin in her hands. "I suppose Alice could use some siblings."

His face didn't change, but she felt the tension in him ebb.

She sat up. "But I'm sure there are plenty of other women who—"

"I don't want other women," he said, firm. "I want you."

She took a deep breath, feeling the weight of the decision she was making. "I know but—"

Mason shook his head. "Don't do it."

She stared at him surprised. "What?"

He held her gaze. "Try to talk yourself out of this."

She bit her lip and took a deep breath. He was right. She would go after what she wanted. She looked around once more and her gaze fell on her aquarium. It was time to finally use it again. She wouldn't run. She wouldn't hide. She wanted to spend the rest of her life with this man. "I'm scared to be this happy. I'm afraid something is going to take it away."

"Nothing is going to take it away," Mason said, his words a promise. "I won't let it."

CHAPTER FORTY-SIX

He's back.

Mason stood in his study and stared at Tracy's text feeling his body grow numb.

Gavin had returned. His stepbrother would disappear for months on end sending Celeste pictures from his travels to wherever the mood struck until he got bored and decided to return to his Maryland condo without warning. Tracy always managed to alert him when that happened.

I expected that.

News of his engagement had already reached his grandmother. She and Celeste were already making plans, although he'd warned them that Julia had to be involved too. He didn't think it would take long for Gavin to find out. He'd been right.

He glanced at the engagement ring Julia had bought him. A white gold band that she'd teased him had cost her all of her savings to find since she needed one big enough.

Bet you Emilia told him. I didn't.

Gavin would want to meet Julia. Mason told himself it didn't matter. That Julia was different. That the past wouldn't repeat itself. He had nothing to worry about.

He was still worried.

It's okay.

No, it's not. What should I do?

Nothing.

Julia can't meet him.

She has to meet him sometime. I trust her.

Me too. I don't trust HIM.

His stepbrother could be a pain, but Emilia had fallen for him because of his charm. It hadn't been on purpose. People just liked Gavin better. That was always how it had been. He had to trust Julia. That she cared about him enough.

Mason began to text a reply when he saw a flash of grey in the corner of his eye. He looked out his window and saw his brother's unassuming grey Mazda drive up. Few people knew that the four door sedan was equipped with an engine that could go from zero to sixty in five seconds. There were many things about Gavin that people didn't see at first glance.

He's here. Mason texted. *I'll talk to him. It will be fine.*

Keep him away from Julia.

Mason smiled finding the request ridiculous. *They have to meet eventually.*

He couldn't keep them apart, but he'd prepare her. He'd...

Mason stiffened when he saw another car drive up. Julia's.

His heart began to pound. He'd forgotten she was coming over to take pictures of Alice.

Maybe Gavin wouldn't see her. His car was parked farther up the drive.

Maybe they'd miss each other.

Mason watched his brother step out of the car, the light autumn wind toying with the dark red scarf he had stylishly draped around his neck. He headed up the main path.

A few more yards and he'd be at the front door.

He hadn't seen her.

Mason looked down when his cell phone alerted him to a text. *Invite her for lunch and introduce him then.*

Mason glanced up and saw his brother turn his head. He watched him stiffen as if in surprise. Mason followed Gavin's attention and saw Julia rummaging through something in her trunk. The wind that had so kindly toyed with his brother's scarf had instead pulled strands of hair from Julia's ponytail, causing them to sway around her head. It also caused her paisley skirt to cling to her legs in an alluring fashion.

Mason shifted his gaze back to Gavin. His stepbrother at first moved slowly then picked up his pace as he headed straight for Julia.

Mason sighed, the feeling of numbness thickening. He replied to his cousin. *It's too late.*

Too late for what?

Keeping them apart.

"Here, let me help you with that."

Julia turned surprised by the warm tone offering to help her with her small cooler. Along with her camera equipment, she'd packed two cartons of pumpkin ice cream—one with tiny chunks of graham crackers and one without—for Mason and herself. She turned to say 'thank you' but when she did the words came out in a breathless rush.

The man who seemed to have materialized beside her took her breath away. He was beautiful. Like an angel with the sunlight taking extra special care to polish his coffee skin, highlight the golden specks in his brown eyes, the sweeping curve of his jaw, the symmetry of every fine feature.

She handed him her camera bag without thinking and closed the trunk. It was when he turned and she was no longer dazzled by the look of him that she realized her mistake. She *never* let anyone carry her camera bag. "Oh, sorry," she said, snatching the bag from his hand before he could argue. "You can carry this instead," she said, holding out the cooler.

She saw a flash of irritation cross his face before a soft smile touched his lips.

It was the smile that caused a shiver of unease to sweep through her. It was haughty and a little mean. Or maybe it was the brief irritation that had colored her thoughts about him. Was he annoyed that she'd given him the cooler instead? It wasn't as heavy as the camera bag; he might have considered it an insult.

But in an instant he wasn't as amazing. At that moment she saw him in a new way. She noticed how he stood just a shade too close to her, enough that his hand twice brushed against the back of hers, but not enough to be alarming. It could have been accidental or by design, although she couldn't think of a reason why he'd want to touch her. But she now realized that the manner in which he'd reached for her camera bag hadn't given her a chance to rebuff him.

They walked a few feet before he paused, slapped his forehead and turned to her. "Where are my manners? I was raised better than that. My mother would—" He stopped and shivered with mock fear. "Never mind. It's terrifying to think about." He held out his hand. "I'm Gavin by the way. Mason's step-brother."

Julia laughed at the expression on his face, imagining that one of Celeste's scoldings would inspire fear. She shook his hand. "I'm Julia, his—"

"His fiancée," Gavin said with a note of amusement,

the haughty smile now gone and replaced with kind interest. "I know. I've heard wonderful things."

"I hope they're not exaggerations."

His beautiful gaze swept over her face. "So far they're all true."

She felt her face burn. He was very personable and easy to talk to. It was almost heady to have such an attractive man shower her with such attention. Only Mason ever looked at her like that.

She lowered her gaze and noticed that he still held her hand. That surprised her. She hadn't noticed it, but he'd held her hand a tiny bit longer than needed. She pulled her hand free and lifted her gaze to his face again. Yes, he was beautiful, but the golden specks in his eyes no longer appeared as charming as they'd once been.

She laughed again, this time from a growing uneasiness. "Well, we'll see how long that lasts." She started walking again, the front door suddenly feeling very far away.

"Are you calling me a liar?" he said in a soft voice.

She spun around surprised by the question. "No, of course not."

His face broke into a smile. "Good." He lifted up the cooler. "What's in here anyway?"

Julia hesitated confused by his changing expressions —she couldn't tell whether he was serious or not. "Pumpkin ice cream."

"I love ice cream. Can I get a taste?"

"Sure," she said. She'd made enough. "But Mason gets the first bite since I made it for him."

An expression—quick, dark, and ugly—swept over his

face before his smile returned. "Then I'm sure it's delicious." He brushed past her and for a moment Julia didn't move as a sinking realization gripped her.

Mason had all the appearance of danger, but something about Gavin told her that although he didn't look dangerous he truly was.

CHAPTER FORTY-EIGHT

Sleeping with her ex probably wasn't one of the smartest things Emilia had ever done, but neither was marrying him either. Gavin was a charming bastard who'd shattered her heart and ruined her life but he'd given her a daughter she loved and Bonnie adored him. Anytime he reentered their lives he came bearing gifts. This time Bonnie beamed with joy when Gavin presented her with a travel helicopter roomy enough for her and two of her dolls. It also had bright seatbelts, controls to play with and a spinnable rotor. It was only due to Mason's help that Bonnie even had a playroom big enough to hold the item.

The thought of her daughter's joy made her heart ache. Gavin was a master of grand gestures, which was why she'd married him. He'd convinced her to sign a contract before their marriage, convincing her that it would protect them both, but assuring her that it wouldn't be a problem because he'd never divorce her.

Because of his lies, when he did leave her, Emilia got no alimony, and a minimum amount of child's support. However, to her daughter he would always be the best dad in the world.

And to Emilia's annoyance he was still the best lover. Her body hummed from remembered pleasure. She watched Gavin as he stood by the side of the bed and buttoned up his shirt.

She took Gavin's pillow and gathered it close, inhaling the scent of rosewood and basil, and sighed in longing, wishing he wanted to stay a little longer. The sex had been amazing, it always was, but she'd regret it later.

Much later when she had time to be alone and think. She didn't want to think and realize she only wanted him in her bed because she didn't want to be lonely. But as she looked at him now, she knew that she may not be alone but she felt lonelier than ever. It had always been that way with him. She could be with him and feel like she was part of the furniture.

She remembered when he'd once held her in his arms and promised her the moon and she believed him. She believed every lie that fell from his lips. If she wasn't careful she could believe them again. He was that kind of man, with that kind of influence. In more ways than one he got better with age.

"So what do you think of her?" he asked.

Emilia didn't need to guess who he was referring to. There was only one reason he'd decided to make a reappearance and it wasn't for her or Bonnie. "I think Mason will get bored of her."

Gavin sent her a look of pity. "That's a wish not an assessment. Let me tell you what I think. I think she's—"

She pushed his pillow from her. "I don't care." But she did. Too much. She didn't want to hear about Julia.

Gavin clicked his tongue. He came around to her side and sat on the edge of the bed. She saw his hand disappear under the sheet then felt its slow sexy ascent up her thigh. "Jealousy doesn't look good on you."

His touch renewed a dormant longing. "I'm not jealous."

"I learned a lot about her during our little ice cream lunch."

Emilia frowned. What was it with that woman and having ice cream as a main meal? "I don't care." She undid one of the buttons on Gavin's shirt, wondering if she could convince him to return to bed. "I'm glad you're here even if it's to cause trouble."

Gavin glanced down as she undid a second button, but made no move to stop her. "Now why would I do that?"

She pressed her hand against his bare chest. "Because that's what you do."

He laughed. "You sound like my mother. She warned me to behave myself." He sniffed. "As if that's even possible," he said then sighed. "Sometimes the way she looks at me you'd think she didn't like me very much."

Emilia could tell that didn't affect him at all. Few things bothered him the way one would think they should.

"Don't upset her."

Gavin sent her a knowing look. "You're the one who contacted me."

She also wondered if that had been a mistake. But Gavin would have found out anyway. Celeste was so happy she would have told him. Nothing that happened would be her fault. *If* anything happened...

Emilia sat up curious. "What are you really planning?"

Gavin shook his head, his gaze heated. "I never plan, I just watch things happen."

Before she could think about what she was doing, sleeping with him again, letting him close, he captured her mouth with his, keeping loneliness at bay for one more night.

CHAPTER FORTY-NINE

"What do you think of Gavin?" Mason asked Julia. They sat together at her computer while she worked on an image she'd taken of Alice. Mason always enjoyed being in her apartment and watching her use a tablet and stylus to ad artistic touches to her work, but it had been nearly two weeks since she'd met his brother and she hadn't said anything.

Julia kept her gaze on the computer screen. "Why do you keep asking me that?"

"Because you keep changing the subject."

"I do not." She pointed to the screen. "I'm going to change the background just for fun, what do you think?"

"You're doing it again."

"What?"

"Changing the subject."

She shrugged. "Doesn't matter what I think. I'm not marrying him."

"But I'm curious."

Julia turned to him. She cupped his face in her hands and placed a light kiss on his lips. "I think he's lucky to have you as a brother." She turned back to the computer.

He felt as if he could breathe again. Gavin was back and Julia hadn't changed. She didn't seem especially surprised by the difference between them. Most people couldn't help but point it out. "I don't want you to feel awkward around him because—"

"He stole the woman you loved."

Mason frowned. "It wasn't like that. They both fell in love with each other. It couldn't be helped." He leaned forward when she mumbled something he couldn't understand. "Sorry?"

"I said you're very forgiving," Julia said, but something about the expression on her face made him wonder if she'd censored what she'd really said.

"It's in the past and I want you to be as comfortable with my family as I am with yours." He'd finally had a chance to have a formal lunch with her mother and sister (he'd met her mother's new husband another time) and enjoyed both women immensely, to Julia's shock.

She shook her head in memory. "I still can't believe my mother only insulted me once."

"She didn't insult you at all."

Julia lifted her nose and mimicked her mother's Jamaican accent. "What's this? Did you get prettier? You must have finally listened to me and tried the juice cleanse I told you about. Your skin glows."

"That's not an insult."

Julia opened her mouth then sighed. "Never mind."

"I liked them."

"And they *loved* you." She sent him a sly glance. "Especially Myla."

Mason couldn't stop a smile. He really enjoyed talking with her. Myla's love of plants was as passionate as his. It was rare to find someone who had such a depth of knowledge and was so easy to talk to.

"Are you sure you're marrying the right sister?" Julia teased him.

Mason rubbed his chin, pensive. "I'm not sure anymore. Her thoughts on allogamy were truly illuminating."

Julia narrowed her eyes. "Why does that sound dirty?"

"It is in a way. It's cross-fertilization. However, I wasn't quite sure of her opinions on autogamy or self-fertilization, an event that occurs in hermaphroditic organisms—"

Julia covered her ears. "Enough. You two were almost inseparable." She let her hands fall and returned her gaze to the screen. "Maybe your brother *is* a better option."

Mason felt his heart grow cold until he saw a tiny smile soften her lips. The sight of it quickly dissolved any lingering fears. She loved him, she was his completely. She was as likely to fall for his stepbrother as he was for her sister.

"Have you gotten to the bottom of finding out the person selling my work?"

"I'm still working on it," he said, but that wasn't quite true.

He'd tracked down her former teacher, but the trail didn't end with him and by following the money he was led down a winding trail that ended somewhere he'd never expected.

"So you have no idea who it is?"

"Not yet," he said in no hurry to tell her the truth because the truth was worst than they could have imagined.

CHAPTER FIFTY

For a man who looked like an angel, he lived like a pig.

Celeste scrunched her nose in distaste as she lifted up a pair of drawers from between her son's sofa cushions. She'd already had to walk over an empty wine glass, push away a pile of clothes before reaching the living room. She gently placed the drawers on the ground and took a seat, facing her son who sat in a loveseat with his arms stretched out the length of it. Looking at him was only a shade better than looking at his messy condo.

"I bet you have more clothes on the floor than in your closet," she said.

Gavin smiled, pleased. "You'd probably win that bet," he said without concern. He made a careless gesture to the room. "Fortunately, that's what maids are for." He tilted his head to the side. "So mother dear, to what do I owe this visit?"

Celeste let her gaze sweep the room once more. Her

son had never been tidy, but there was a renewed carelessness to how he'd tossed things. As if he were upset about something. Part of her was thrilled because she knew why. It was the reason she'd come to see him. "You have to stop."

"Stop what?"

"Twice you've asked Julia out to lunch."

He shrugged. "It was a friendly gesture."

"Another time you asked her to dinner and you've also dropped by her place."

"I had some question about her work. Did Mason complain?"

"No, Julia did."

Celeste bit back a grin when she saw the shock in his eyes. He hadn't expected to meet someone immune to his charms. The expression quickly disappeared as his expressions always did. "I didn't realize she was so sensitive."

"I think you may have met someone who won't fall for you."

He rubbed the back of his neck, amused. "It will just take time." He tilted his head back. "When she first met me, she could hardly breathe."

"Possibly because you were sucking up all the oxygen."

"That's cute, but there's no use pretending." Gavin leaned forward, his gaze darkening. "You wouldn't be here, if you weren't worried."

"I'm not worried. I'm ashamed. I'm ashamed that I raised such a greedy man who can't stand seeing his brother happy."

"You're always taking his side."

"Leave Julia alone. You have so much. Let Mason have this."

"Why should I? I let him have you, didn't I?" He folded his arms. "I had to sit by and watch you dote over him. Everyone doted over him after they stopped being afraid. I don't know why."

"He has something you don't. A heart."

Gavin sniffed. "They're not very useful. Hearts can be broken or stolen. I prefer stealing myself, much more entertaining. It's not my fault if my stepbrother is dumb enough to let a woman steal his heart. He should be more careful."

Celeste's voice hardened. "You always wanted whatever Mason had. I wish—"

"Remember when you tried to warn me off Emilia?" He flashed a wistful grin. "You told me how she and Mason were perfect for each other. That you'd convinced him to take a chance with her." He tapped the side of his forehead. "What was it that you said to me again? You talked about how he deserved love after losing his dad." He paused. "Yet you never once asked me about losing mine."

"Because your father isn't dead."

"You act like he is. You never talk about him. It's always Ernest."

"Ernest raised you. He gave you more than your father ever did."

"That may be true." His words turned to ice. "But he had the same flaw you did. He favored Mason. Mason was the quiet, sensitive one who everyone misunderstood. *I* was the one with loads of friends, my grades were as high as his, sometimes even higher, I—"

"Couldn't get enough. We could never give you enough attention. Enough praise. None of this is about Mason. It's about you realizing you have nothing to offer but your looks and hollow flattery."

It hurt her to say the words. As despicable as he was, she still loved her son. Still wished there was potential to reach him and help him become a better man. A better human being.

And for a moment, when she saw a tiny spark of hurt then anger in his gaze, she hoped that she would be able to help him take a different path. But soon the cunning smile returned and she knew she had lost him. "Perhaps you're right. I'm a lost cause."

She shook her head. "I didn't say that."

"No. You didn't need to." He slowly rose to his feet. "So I'll do exactly what I want to do."

"I'm warning you."

He bent down and placed a kiss on her cheek. Unlike Mason's soft quick pecks, Gavin's always hurt a little. "Warn away," he whispered in her ear. "It makes the game more fun."

CHAPTER FIFTY-ONE

Nolan swore when he entered his office one late afternoon and found Mason sitting at Julia's desk. The big, hard-faced man was the last person he wanted to see today. He couldn't understand how his daughter could have fallen in love with him. Let alone wanted to marry him. But he did have money. That would be a plus for both of them in the future, if he played his cards right.

"Julia give you a key?" Nolan said, tapping down his anger as he walked to his desk.

Mason jangled his keys in the air. "Yes, in case of an emergency. She also let me know that you like to work here on your own after office hours."

Nolan sat behind his desk. "So why are you here? I'm doing everything you told me to."

Mason nodded and swung side to side in Julia's new swivel chair. "You've made Julia very happy recently."

"So what's the problem?"

"The last few weeks I've been working on a puzzle.

But a lot of pieces didn't fit. But first I have to talk about something that's been bothering me. Your debt to my mother. It didn't make sense to me that you would be so easily conned by a couple you'd just met. Didn't even know. Why would you vouch for them so thoroughly? It also didn't make sense that you would carry such a large debt without telling your daughter. You're used to her getting you out of trouble. What made this different?"

"The amount. I felt like such a fool."

"I thought so too, until I tracked down the couple whose wedding you paid for. They weren't as hard to find as you made out and they were very chatty. You weren't strangers to each other. The woman was blackmailing you. She discovered you'd convinced Julia's teacher to do the gallery showings. He didn't see much in her work. He saw trash, but you saw a goldmine. That's when you came up with your plan."

Nolan shook his head. "That's ridiculous."

"Using a fake name you formed another business and through that company started to license her work in secret. You never suspected that someone would make a connection to you, but then someone did. It was just bad luck on your part. You were very clever to do most of your business aboard. What you didn't expect was a small Jamaican B&B to purchase one of Julia's photos and have a former classmate of Julia's stay there and ask about the work.

"To her shock, the owner told her that the photographer was dead. This woman did a search and while yes, Della, was dead and had an extensive history online, the true photographer, Julia Lester, was very much alive. She didn't think Julia would fake her death to sell her work, so her mind began spinning."

Nolan grinned. "And this is a funny tale you're spinning, but it's only a story."

"But the story doesn't end. Seeing an opportunity, this woman first contacts her former teacher. He doesn't know what she is talking about, so she hazards a guess. Who else close to Julia could pull this off? That question led her to you. She blackmailed you. You panicked and thought that the extravagant wedding would be payment enough. But it wasn't. She kept coming back. That's why, recently, you've been telling Julia about clients who haven't paid, why the company keeps losing money."

Mason pointed at him. "That was another thing that bothered me. Your wife, excuse me *ex*-wife, once told me you were a cheapskate and that got me to thinking about your desk and equipment and even the townhouse. A cheapskate cares about money. They wouldn't keep being conned by clients. They would make sure to get at least some payment. Especially someone like you who takes pride in his work. But I also learned that you'd been an engineer. What engineer would build a system that kept leaking money? It didn't make sense.

"So I looked a little closer at your bookkeeping, with Julia's permission of course, and thought about how engineers like to build redundancies into systems. Something as a backup, like a spare tire in a car. And I discovered that you'd built one too. A system that allowed you to siphon money without Julia ever knowing.

"You had a second accounting software that tracked all your clients and projects. The difference was that all the clients had paid in full. But Julia didn't know this because although you pretended not to care about money and let her handle most things, you kept control of the finances. Business wasn't as bad as she thought it was. You were doing other events Julia didn't know about and was getting great referrals. That's how the Hartwells found you." Mason held up his hand. "Don't lie. I spoke to them."

Nolan closed his mouth.

"However, you were going through money trying to keep two businesses going, one whose income stream was starting to dry up due to lack of planning, plus a blackmailer. It couldn't last, so you created a form specifically for Julia to see that had three phony clients that Julia would see hadn't paid. Those bogus clients would convince her that possibly others hadn't paid either and that's why the company was suffering. Did you pay actors to play the role when she contacted them?"

Nolan didn't move.

"I also wondered about your panic attacks. Julia told me they'd happened recently, only a few years ago. She blamed the divorce, not knowing you were being blackmailed and that these attacks were growing worse the more and more you felt trapped in a corner."

Nolan gripped his hands on the desk.

"But the final item that kept bothering me, the puzzle piece I had to fit, was the look on your face when I first saw you. You thought I was a thug. You were scared but not surprised. That was strange. Why would you be expecting a criminal if you hadn't dealt with one before?

Maybe you had. That made me wonder what you'd been hiding. And now I know."

Nolan surged to his feet. "You can't tell Julia. I've been paying this woman all these years because I don't want her to know. It was a moment of weakness. I haven't done anything since. I swear. You can't tell her."

"I have to. I promised I wouldn't lie—"

"You don't have to lie. Don't say anything. If you do, you'll ruin everything. This will hurt her more than..." He paused. "When her mother and I separated she was never quite the same. Do you think she'll thank you for telling her about this?"

Mason shook his head. "She deserves—"

"Do you think she'll be happy starting a family with the very man who disgraced her father?" Nolan took a deep breath. "Listen to me. I know Julia. If I can turn the business around everything will be fine. If you can help me with the blackmailers—"

"You don't have to worry about the blackmailers anymore," Mason said in a soft voice.

His eyes widened. "Did you—"

Mason frowned. "I don't kill people. And I didn't do anything to them. I didn't have to. They got overconfident with you. Too confident. After my little chat with the woman she and her husband decided to blackmail a wealthier target. Unfortunately, they found someone who would rather see them dead than negotiate. They are now on the run."

Nolan breathed a sigh of relief. "Then it's perfect. Julia never has to know. This can stay between us. It's the best for her. It's the best for you if you don't want to lose her."

Mason gritted his teeth. The thought filled him with fear. "All right."

"Thank you."

Mason stood. "Don't thank me."

Nolan lowered his gaze and said in a quiet voice. "I've made a lot of mistakes, but I do love my daughter you know."

Mason stood. "Now it's time to show it."

CHAPTER FIFTY-TWO

He was lying again and he didn't like it.

Mason slid off his engagement ring and placed it on his desk with a soft click. He didn't deserve it. Not when he wasn't the man she thought he was. Twice Julia had asked him about his investigation and he'd given her vague replies. He wasn't sure how long he could keep it up.

He'd wait until after the wedding. Just a few more months and then he'd tell her. But then again, she may not forgive him. Perhaps he could come up with a story that would satisfy her and cause her to stop asking questions.

"Nolan was right," he said to Alice who was happily chatting and whistling away to a classical rap song Julia had given him. The bird seemed to have found a new favorite musical genre but Mason was in no mood to play with her. "I don't want to lose her," he said to himself. He was too close to getting everything he wanted. He walked to the window and thought of the years he'd spent alone with only Alice as company. He didn't want to go back to that. If he had to lie to keep her close, keep her safe, he would.

He had to.

"How quaint," someone said behind him. "An engagement ring."

Mason turned and saw Gavin holding up the ring he'd left on his desk.

Gavin flashed a cruel grin. "Is she going to buy you a dress as well?"

"Put it down."

Alice flapped her wings. "Mic drop!"

Gavin studied the ring. "How much do you think she spent?"

"I said put it down."

"How does she like being second choice? Then again she looks like she's used to it so you're lucky there."

"I won't ask you a third time."

Gavin slid the ring in his trouser pocket. "And what if I don't? What are you going to do?" He sauntered towards Mason with a superior grin on his face. "Hit me? We both know you won't do that." He stopped a few feet in front of him. "Because the big ox can't fight. He gets woozy at the sight of blood." Gavin turned. "Does she know you're pathetic?"

Mason grabbed the back of Gavin's shirt and twisted it in his fist like a tourniquet. Gavin scratched at his arms, scrambling to free himself. But Mason ignored his choking gurgles. He retrieved the ring from his stepbrother's pocket before he shoved him away.

Gavin grabbed his neck and gasped for air. He glared at him.

Mason slid the ring on his finger unmoved. "You shouldn't have turned your back on me."

Tracy entered the room. "What's taking so long? You were supposed to tell him that the dinner was ready."

Mason swore he'd forgotten he'd offered to host Julia, Tracy, Celeste, Emilia, Bonnie and Gavin for dinner. He couldn't even remember the last time he'd had so many guests. He didn't want to disappoint them. Soon he'd invite Julia's family too, but he was taking small steps.

Gavin pointed at him. "I started to but then he tried to kill me."

Tracy clapped her hands. "Bravo."

Gavin sent her a scorching look. "I'm serious."

"So am I." She went over to Mason, tugged on his collar so she could place a kiss on his cheek.

"I'm the wounded hero," Gavin said affronted. "Don't I deserve a kiss?" He tapped his own cheek.

Tracy frowned. "I'd rather suffer a yeast infection."

He chuckled. "Fortunately other women don't feel that way."

"Booyah!" Alice said before she gave a catcall whistle.

Gavin grinned. "See? Even birds love me."

"Only because you taught her that," Tracy said.

He headed for the door. "I wonder if I should tell Julia that you're still in love with Emilia."

"Go ahead," Tracy said. "She won't believe you."

He shifted his gaze from Tracy to Mason then back again. "Somehow I think she will."

He left the room.

Tracy grabbed Mason's arm before he could follow him. "Don't listen to him. He's wrong. Julia loves you. He's not a threat. You're not going to lose her this time."

Mason looked down at his engagement ring, weighted by the secret he had to keep, desperate to believe her.

CHAPTER FIFTY-THREE

Under a cool dark sky of an autumn evening, Mason carried a sleeping Bonnie to Emilia's car. To his relief the dinner had gone well. Gavin had tried to tease and goad Julia about Mason's past relationship with Emilia but she seemed unaffected, focusing on Tracy and Celeste, and he soon lost interest. Mason felt completely at ease after that, his mother did too, strangely enough, and the evening ended faster than expected. Gavin left first then Tracy so Mason offered to help Emilia with Bonnie.

"You don't really want to do this," Emilia said, opening the backdoor of her car.

"Do what?"

"Marry her."

Mason shook his head. He gently placed Bonnie in her car seat. "Don't do this." He glanced back at the house wondering if anyone was watching. "You'll give Julia the wrong idea."

"No, I won't. She'll see exactly what I want her to."

He fastened Bonnie in her seat before he quietly shut the door. "Drive home safe." He turned.

Emilia grabbed his arm. "I mean it. You're only thinking of marrying her because you don't want to be alone."

He yanked his arm free. "Go home, Emilia."

Her voice became urgent. "Remember the night you asked me to marry you?"

Too well. "Why bring that up?"

"Because *you* didn't ask to marry her, *she* asked you. That's what you told Celeste." When he hesitated she smiled. "The thought of marriage didn't even cross your mind. You wouldn't have thought of it if she hadn't asked you first."

"That's not—"

"You wouldn't have because you don't love her the way you loved me. You're both so different. It might seem novel now but in time the difference will grow." She took his hand. "But not with us. We fit. You know that." He pulled away. "Emilia, stop this."

"I made a mistake." Her voice shook. "Do I have to keep paying for it? Why will you punish us because of your pride? You don't love her the way you love me. You think I haven't noticed how you've looked at me over the years?" She grabbed the front of his jacket. "How much you've wanted me? I know you love me Mason. You still love me. You're the kind of man who doesn't stop loving."

Mason took a deep breath. He removed her grip on his shirt and held her cool hands in his. "You're right. I do love you." He bit his lip seeing the joy in her gaze. "But I don't want to marry you." He paused, watching her eyes pool with unshed tears. "I love Julia and I am going to marry her. I need you to accept that. There's no second chance for us. There doesn't need to be. There's someone else out there for you. Move on."

Her gaze held his, pleading. "And if I don't?"

"You will because deep down you know I'm right. You're clinging to a past you made up in your mind. You don't love me. Never have."

"I do. Why won't you believe me?"

He let her hands fall. "Maybe you did love me once. Maybe you do love me now."

"Yes, I do."

"But you'll get bored of me, just as you did back then. You went out with me because I was the safe choice your family expected you to choose, but you didn't want that. You wanted the excitement Gavin offered. You're only clinging to me now because it feels safe. But you don't need that. You don't need me. You're a beautiful, intelligent woman. Gavin made you forget that. There are a number of men who would be lucky to meet you and capture your heart. I'm not that man."

She stepped away from him, angrily wiping away tears. "It doesn't seem fair." She looked up at the castle touched by the moonlight. "Julia gets all that I'd dreamed of: A career she loves, a beautiful home and a man who adores her. She's so happy." Emilia looked at him. "You are too. I envy that."

"Do you remember what you said to me when you turned down my proposal?"

Emilia shook her head, sad. "Please don't."

"You said you couldn't love me the way you should. You said that I deserved better. You were never more right. When Julia came into my life I realized that I deserved someone who loved me for who I am. Don't be fooled. Julia may have asked me to marry her first, but the truth is I was already completely hers."

CHAPTER FIFTY-FOUR

The new camera bag was a bad sign.

Julia had been talking about buying one for years. Her father said when he won the lottery he'd get it for her. The price for the expensive camera bag alone had become a joke between them.

But now it sat on her office desk.

Instead of joy the sight of it filled her with dread. The last time her father had bought her an extravagant gift, a new coat she'd been eying for months, was the day before he announced he and her mother were separating.

Julia shook her head, wearied and concerned. She didn't want gifts if he was hiding something from her. "Dad, I don't want—"

"Just take it." He sent her a look. "Consider it an early wedding present."

She set the bag on the ground and sat behind her desk. "Tell me everything."

She expected him to look shocked, outraged,

confused. But instead a look of embarrassment then shame crossed his features before he said with anger, "Don't pretend you don't know. You always act like you know everything, why stop now?"

She stiffened hoping not to give her shock away. She didn't know what he was talking about, but didn't want him to know that. "Okay. I won't lecture you."

"When did Mason tell you?" Her father tapped his chest. "You may have heard his side of things, but did you ever think to listen to mine?"

What was Mason supposed to have told her? What side did she have to listen to? "Go ahead," Julia said ready to hear everything.

"I should have known Mason would tell you. I thought he was better than that. I thought he loved you and wanted to protect you as much as I did, but I was wrong. I thought he was a man I could trust." Her father stood, walked over to her desk and pressed his palms flat on it. "But I can explain. Setting up the company and selling your work was never my initial aim. I wanted to try it out and see how people would respond to your work without you knowing. I didn't want to see you hurt in case it failed. But the sales happened so fast and they were offering good money for your work. It was supposed to be a surprise. I told you your work was good."

He'd never told her that. Not years ago and certainly not now. But she was too shocked to argue with him.

He licked his lower lip and stroked his beard. "But I'm not the best with business and contracts and I got involved with blackmailers who threatened your life if I ever revealed the truth that you were alive. Your work was more valued if you were dead and they—"

Julia stared at him open-mouthed. "You were being blackmailed?"

"Yes, that's why I had to create the phony clients..." His words faded. He stumbled back from her desk, realization crossing his face. "Mason didn't tell you anything, did he?"

"No."

"I'm sorry, but I had to do what I did. I had no choice."

"You had to steal my work?"

"Yes!" he said with feeling. "Because you stole my dream!"

"What?"

He gripped his hand into a fist, his words turned bitter. "I've always loved photography. I introduced you to it, but it was my love first. But nobody responded to my work the way they did yours. They didn't respond to the pure art of what I captured, they wanted manipulated software and digital art."

"Most people couldn't understand them," she said remembering how poorly the turn out for her gallery showings were.

"Exactly, but you let them just sit there doing nothing when they could make money. In a way I helped you. I let your work get seen, their notoriety wouldn't have gotten this far without me."

Julia shook her head, disappointed. "You really believe that?"

He pointed at her. "Don't look at me like that. Everything comes easy to you."

She jumped to her feet. "Easy?"

"Yes. You have no idea how hard it is to fight to not be a failure. My marriage failed, my business nearly failed, my dream..." He sighed. "I couldn't let that fail too. I needed this tiny success. You didn't. I was desperate to have something to prove to your mother she was wrong about me."

"If that were true, why did you keep it a secret?"

He hesitated. "I told you." He wrung his hands together. "I got in too deep and was being blackmailed by dangerous people. Our lives, *your* life was in danger, that's why Mason had to get involved. You're lucky to have a rich man who will—"

"Sweep in and save the day because I'm a clueless woman who gets everything she wants?"

"That came out wrong."

Julia glared at him. "Everything you've said is wrong. I didn't steal anything from you. You're the one who decided to do wedding photography."

"Because I had no choice! We needed the money and *you* said people would always get married and need someone to capture it."

Julia nodded. "You're also the one who decided *not* to take the evening class with me even though I told you. You could have learned new photography techniques and styles. I even showed you a class online you could try but you refused. You gave up on your dream long ago. You can't blame anyone else for that."

Her father shook his head, looking sad and much older. "That's where you're wrong."

Julia stared at him not knowing how to feel. She hadn't meant to cause her father pain. She'd never thought that her dreams were, in anyway, a threat to his. All these years she'd helped him and he'd secretly despised.

She slowly sank back into her seat. Hurt was too simple a word to describe her feelings. Anger didn't work either. She felt a pain from something she couldn't name and it seemed to squeeze every part of her, made her feel both hard and brittle at the same time. Part of her felt foolish. Shouldn't she feel a little proud that her work was getting seen? That someone had paid for it? Did getting credit really matter?

But then she realized it wasn't about credit, it was the betrayal. It was the bitterness that had tinged her father's words, the anger in his eyes. The anger she'd never seen before. She had thought they were close, that he depended on her.

She didn't know who she was without him. After her parents' separation so much of her identity had been to shore him up, to stroke his ego, to make the business a success and now all those efforts felt useless, fruitless.

But the worse part of it all what that Mason knew...

CHAPTER FIFTY-FIVE

Mason gripped his cell phone as he stood at his study window. A dusting of snow covered the ground. He'd been looking forward to Julia's phone call. He enjoyed talking to her about their plan to turn the stone cottage into her studio. But Julia's question filled him with dread.

"Mason," Julia insisted when he remained silent. "How long did you know?"

He headed for the door. "Where are you?"

"How long?"

She wasn't supposed to find out like this. She was never supposed to know. He had to reach her. He had to see her in person. "We need to talk about this."

"How long?"

He stopped in the doorway and sighed. "Several weeks."

"So when I asked you if you knew who was behind

everything and you said you didn't know you were lying, right?"

He hesitated. "I wasn't sure at first, but then—"

"You found out the truth," she finished.

"Yes."

"And you lied to me."

He bit his lip. "Julia, I—"

"You promised. You promised never to lie to me."

Mason rested his forehead against the wall and closed his eyes. "I didn't want to see you get hurt. I wanted to protect you. I honestly wasn't sure you'd believe me."

"So you lied to me over and over again?"

"I didn't want to."

"But you did," she said in a flat voice. "How can you expect me to trust you now?"

Because I did it all for you. Because I love you. "If you'll let me explain."

"I don't care."

He squeezed his eyes tight, fighting tears. He'd heard that tone before. It was the same one Emilia had used when she'd told him she was in love with someone else. It was the tone of goodbye. *Please don't leave me*, he wanted to tell her, but he knew it would be useless. "I'm sorry."

"Me too. I'm sorry I ever thought—" He heard her take a shaky breath. "This is the last time I let you hurt me. I never want to see you again."

CHAPTER FIFTY-SIX

She got rid of the aquarium.

She ignored calls from her mom.

Texts from her sister.

Knocks on the door when Chloe stopped by.

Instead Julia disappeared into books.

In one week she read twenty.

The following week she read thirty-five.

She didn't take pictures. She could hear the bitterness in her father's voice every time she lifted the camera. He'd not only stolen her work, he'd stolen the joy of photography from her.

Tracy sent flowers. Julia gave them away.

She even received a message from Mason's grandmother. Her tone was haughty but Julia could hear fear in her voice.

It was Celeste's tearful plea that shook her the most. Julia deleted the message before it finished, unable to listen to Celeste telling her about how Mason had had to cope with the loss of his father.

Mason wasn't the only one who'd suffered a loss.

In a way she'd lost a father too. Perhaps she'd never really had one.

Julia sat on her couch and glared at the stack of books that took the place of the aquarium. Anger roiled within her. Everyone she cared about seemed to be on Mason's side.

Didn't she matter too? Why didn't anyone consider what she felt? Why didn't anyone think about what Mason had truly done to her? She'd forgiven him once for deceiving her. Why should she forgive him again? She wanted someone safe, someone she could trust. Was that too much to ask?

She kept everyone at a distance, trying her best to figure out what she was going to do next. She'd never work with her father again.

Two dreams had shattered: She wouldn't be marrying the man she loved and she wouldn't be starting a new career with his help.

She'd never touch a camera again. She considered working with her mother, although the thought gave her heartburn, until she figured out another option. Working with her mother would be hard, but it was better than Myla's offer to work with her company. Being around so many flowers would only remind her of Mason. She couldn't bear that.

Julia jumped up from her couch and stretched her gaze falling on the ZZ plant. She would be fine without him even though she couldn't get rid of the plants he'd given her yet.

She left her apartment walked down to the main floor to check her mail. She pulled out a stack of junk mail.

"Need help with that?" a familiar voice said.

She turned to Gavin shocked. "I thought you were out of the country."

He held his arms out to the side. "You thought wrong."

"What do you want?" She paused. "Don't tell me Mason sent you."

Gavin shook his head. "Nobody knows I'm here," he said in a conspiratorial whisper. He glanced at the elevators. "Care to invite me up?"

The question sounded harmless, she knew the man was not. "I have a better idea. You can treat me to coffee."

MINUTES later she sat in a café with a man who had three women casting lustful looks at him from a nearby table. A male barista who'd twice forgotten Julia's order, had given Gavin an almond croissant 'on the house' and a large espresso, although he'd asked for a regular.

He sat and talked to her completely unaware of the attention or used to it. He asked her how she was coping with Mason's betrayal, what her plans were for the future and told her if she ever needed anyone to talk to, he was there for her.

Julia looked at his beautiful face and felt instantly better. It was hard to be miserable with a man whose penetrating gaze was intoxicating. Unlike everyone else, he didn't make her feel bad about her choices.

Breaking up with Mason had been the right thing to do. The right thing for her. Gavin's steady gaze made her feel beautiful, smart and strong. She didn't feel foolish with him. His attention was like a drug she could get addicted to. She could see why Emilia had fallen for him. He was good for the ego.

Julia folded her arms. "Enough about me. What about you?"

Gavin lowered his gaze as well as his voice. "What about me?"

"What do you want?"

He shrugged. "Who says I want anything?"

"You must have come to my place for a reason."

His gaze met hers. "Not really. I was in the neighborhood and I was curious."

"About what?"

"You." He rested his chin in his hand and studied her face. "I asked you out plenty of times before. Why did you say yes now?"

She leaned forward and rested her arms on the table. "Perhaps I'm curious about you too."

He began to smile. "I like that. You like taking pictures, right? How about we commemorate this moment and take a picture together?"

"So that you can send it to Mason?"

His smile slowly faded.

His surprise nearly made her laugh. "I'm not Emilia. I'm surprised you hadn't realized that by now, but you're so busy trying to hurt Mason you didn't see it. I came here with you because I was bored and feeling sorry for myself. Not because I'm impressed by you. I'm not so broken hearted that I don't see the kind of man you are."

He sniffed unfazed. "Perhaps. But at least I'm not a hypocrite." He reached into his trouser pocket and pulled out the engagement ring she'd bought for Mason.

She gasped. "What are you doing with that?"

Gavin shrugged. "Who cares? He doesn't have much use for it now." He lifted the ring and read the inscription. "Love you always." He set the ring on its side and spun it in a circle. "But you didn't mean that, did you?" A cruel smile touched his beautiful mouth. "That's why I don't believe in love. He does." Gavin gripped the ring in his fist, his eyes bright with merriment. "And you hurt him more than I ever could. I'm almost jealous."

The thought horrified her. She looked at Gavin's smug face and saw herself.

She had been as selfish as her father. She had only focused on her own hurt and pain. Yes, he had lied. Yes, he had broken a promise. But was it enough to shut him out of her life?

You're the best thing that's ever happened to me. More than you know.

By pushing him away, she was letting her father win. It was his lies, his deceit that had come between her and Mason.

And he'd been the one person who *hadn't* stood up for Mason. Everyone else from Chloe to Celeste to Tracy, even her mother, had tried to make her give Mason a second chance.

But her father never did. He'd never taken blame for

the secret Mason had kept for him. Perhaps, like Gavin, he too was a little jealous. Not just jealous of her skill as a photographer, but that she was embarking on a future without him.

Julia rose to her feet. "Thank you."

Gavin stared up at her surprised. "For what?"

"For showing me what true beauty is." She held out her palm. "Now give me back the ring."

He slowly blinked, challenge in his eyes. "And if I don't?"

CHAPTER FIFTY-SEVEN

He'd leave Wendhaven.

He couldn't imagine staying there without her. He'd let Julia into his inner sanctum and wherever he turned he saw her. He saw her in his bed, sitting at his table, playing with Alice.

Mason walked into his study and paused. Alice was happily whistling to a country song and Julia was sitting in his favorite chair reading.

Julia.

Was sitting.

In his chair.

For a second he didn't move, wondering if he was hallucinating. But she was too real. A hallucination didn't smell like sweetened coffee and mint, it didn't hum in tune to the music, it didn't shift in its seat and cross its legs in a way that made his entire body burn.

Julia closed the book and waved it at him so that he could see the cover: *Return to Love.* "I think it's about time I return this to you." She stood and placed the book back on the shelf, filling the hole that it had left behind.

He wanted to pull her into his arms and hold her. He wanted to taste her lips again and tell her how lost he'd been without her. How truly sorry he was. But he didn't move.

She turned to him. "That's not the only reason I'm here." She walked up to him. He felt his pulse increase with each step, his breath grew shallow. "I have something else to give back to you." She lifted up his hand then held up the engagement ring. "If you still want it."

He gathered her close and whispered against her lips, "All that matters to me is you," before he kissed her. The dark, emptiness that had gripped his life for so long finally faded away. "Marry me."

She slid the ring on his finger. "With pleasure."

He looked down at his hand amazed. "How...where did you get it? I couldn't find it."

"Gavin gave it to me."

His brows shot up. "He *gave* it to you?"

"He needed a little persuading but after I punched him he didn't argue." Julia grinned with wicked delight. "It was great. I hit him in the nose and blood gushed out. I think he got some on his shirt..." Her words fell away when Mason's expression changed. "Never mind. Sit down."

He swallowed. "I'm fine."

"Sit down anyway. You're not allowed to faint."

"I'm not going to faint," he said. He took a deep breath, steadying his senses. This moment was too important to him to lose control. "I'm sorry I hurt you. I had my reasons, but they're not good enough. I'll do whatever it takes to rebuild your trust in me. I'll—"

Julia shook her head. "You don't have to do anything. I already forgive you and I'll keep on forgiving you because you'll make mistakes and so will I. But that's okay. I realized that I don't need to be safe, I just need to be loved."

Mason's gaze held hers, sending a silent vow he intended to keep. "Always."

CHAPTER FIFTY-EIGHT

SIX MONTHS LATER...

Celeste didn't cry at weddings.

When she watched Mason and Julia exchange vows that soft spring day at Wendhaven she didn't shed a tear, although her heart was full of joy.

It was the reception that got her.

The moment they stepped into the Great Hall and she saw a virtual gallery of large images displayed around the room tears sprung to her eyes.

There were tiny captured moments—Bonnie's sleeping face resting on a broad shoulder, a large hand tending to a delicate flower, a budgie perched on a finger, a man in silhouette against a Kenyan sunset.

Even though his face didn't appear in the pictures it was clear every picture was of Mason.

Yes, this was it. Someone had finally captured her stepson's unique beauty. His gentleness and strength. She could feel safe that when she was no longer here there was someone who would care for him, look out for him, love him.

Please look after him, Ernest had asked her. She'd fulfilled her husband's wish.

The room filled with the sound of surprised laughter, she knew it belonged to Mason, but for a moment she heard his father's delight and imagined Ernest there with them.

"She didn't tell me she was doing this," Mason said behind her, resting a hand on her shoulder.

"That's because it was supposed to be a surprise," Julia said, looping her arm through his.

Mason frowned uncertain. "They're huge. You sure they won't scare anyone?"

Tracy rushed over to them. "Julia, I can't believe this is what you were up to. They're amazing!"

She beamed. "Thanks."

"But I thought you didn't like taking pictures of people."

"You're right. I don't." Julia gazed up at Mason, blissfully happy with the man who met her gaze. "I just take pictures of things I love."

ABOUT THE AUTHOR

Dara Girard, an award-winning, national bestselling author of more than forty novels, from romance to suspense, loves telling stories.

Born in the US to immigrant parents, Dara enjoys pulling from her Jamaican, British, Nigerian heritage and exposure to various cultures to bring what reviewers and fans call "vivid emotional stories" to life. She is best known for her popular Henson Series, the mysterious Clifton Sisters, and the fun Black Stockings Society.

You can write her at:
contactdara@daragirard.com
or
P.O. Box 10345
Silver Spring, MD 20914
If you'd like to receive a reply, please send a self-addressed stamped envelope.

Visit her website to sign up for her newsletter and get sneak peeks, monthly updates on new releases, and special offers.

For more information visit
www.daragirard.com